TO GAIN A BODYGUARD

GAINING LOVE NOVELLA

TANYA EAVENSON

To Gain a Bodyguard

ISBN-10: 1-945981-01-6
ISBN-13: 978-1-945981-01-2

ACKNOWLEDGMENTS

I want to thank my husband for his love and support as I continue to write the stories God places on my heart. And thank you to all my readers. I hope you enjoy Brice and Madi's story!

WHAT READERS ARE SAYING

"To Gain a Mommy was a very sweet and heartwarming novella that I did not want to put down. All the characters jumped off the page and felt very real. I absolutely loved this story and would highly recommend it to anyone who loves great contemporary Christian romances!" ~Ashley

"I love reading everything by this author! She brings her stories to life and holds your attention." ~Kris

"I'm so glad I got a chance to read this author's work. She has a wonderful way of writing the characters so that to this day they are still fresh in my mind. The story had some twists to it, which I appreciated, and was believable and relatable. Carl and Hope are such a lovely couple and the supporting cast of children (and a dog!) helped bring humor and life to their relationship. I highly recommend this story for anyone who loves a sweet, feel-good Christian romance." ~Amazon Reviewer

"Another swoonworthy read from Tanya Eavenson! I truly enjoyed this story about Amabelle and Patrick (so glad he got his own happily-ever-after!). The characters were well-developed and the storyline was satisfying and sweet. If you love animals, you'll be pleasantly surprised to find just about every kind of pet possible in this book." ~Amazon Reviewer

"Funny, endearing, romantic. The characters grabbed my heart and made me wish their story could just go on." ~Kindle Customer

Books by Tanya Eavenson

Unconditional
Unending Love Series Book One
Elizabeth wants to forget. Chris wants to save his
marriage. Can they trust God with their future and find a
love that's unconditional?

Restored
Unending Love Series Book Two
Unwilling to deal with his cancer prognosis, Dr. Steven
Moore retreats to a happier time in his past—to the
woman who once stole his heart, never suspecting she
might offer hope for his future.

To Gain a Mommy
Gaining Love Novella Book One
When Hope Michaels decides to face her past, she
unknowingly purchases the house across the street from
her former fiancé—the man her twin sister married, then
widowed. Fire Captain Carl McGuire can put out any
flame, except for the one Hope sparks within him—some
things never change.

To Gain a Valentine
Gaining Love Novella Book Two
As Valentine's Day approaches, will Patrick and Amabelle
miss out on the love they've always desired? Or will their
love take flight under the stars on this very special night?

CHAPTER ONE

The vanity lights from the hotel room accented the highlights in Madi Reynolds' blond curls. Fingering them, she turned her head to the side and practiced an alluring bat of her lashes.

She was an ICE agent for Homeland Security, but first, she was a woman. Today, she would use both to uncover where a local pimp named Prince was hiding the girls he'd bought through a sex-trafficking ring.

Madi had her own girls, also undercover agents, in four major cities. They knew her as Constance. According to intelligence she was a player, but tonight's meeting would be her first reach into Atlanta.

After taking a tissue from the box, she blotted her tawny lips, admiring the lace trim on her neckline where the digital mic would capture her conversations. She inhaled a long breath and tossed the tissue into the waste basket.

From the moment she'd woken, she couldn't shake the feeling something was off. She rehearsed how the next few hours would go—where she'd sit, what she'd say. So much hinged on the outcome of this meeting.

A text came through her cell. *Hey, Madilyn, I'm coming to town and hope to see you before the wedding.*

Why was Asher texting her now?

She muted her phone and ignored the message. Bowing her head, she let a prayer form. *Lord, give me the words, and the—*

Two knocks sounded.

"Amen," she whispered, then put command in her voice. "Who is it?"

"Covington."

"Enter."

The door gave its typical creak as it opened. Brice Johnson stepped into the room, stowing his key card inside his dark jacket.

Madi caught a glimpse of the Glock in his side holster and wished she were wearing hers, but there was little room after she poured herself into this dress.

She met his haunting blue eyes and her heart jarred at the intensity of his gaze. To most, he was a war veteran. Undercover, he was Constance's bodyguard. But to Madi… She wasn't sure what they were to each other.

A look in his expression made her pause.

Whatever was behind those eyes, his gaze had yet to waver, but hers fell away. She reached for the two-carat diamond earrings and slipped them on. "Is everything set?" She lifted the box that held the matching diamond necklace and opened it gently, hoping he couldn't see her nervousness. She was never nervous. What was wrong with her? This meeting was too important. Lives of children were at stake, and she had to play her cards to perfection.

"Everything is set, but there's been a change."

"Oh." She began fastening the necklace, her fingers

fumbling with the clasp.

"You'll be with Agent Scott."

She flinched as Brice took a step closer and slid her long curls over her shoulder.

"I know you've been uncomfortable around him lately, but I need to make sure there aren't any surprises." He took over fastening the necklace.

"How would you know I was uncomfortable?"

"You bite the inside of your lip." He lingered for a moment, then laid her hair along her back. "Madi."

This was the way they were together, him quiet, protective, keeping her at arm's length. She, on the other hand, found herself breathless in his presence, keeping the hope of them alive.

"Yes?" she whispered, afraid her voice would reveal how his simple touch affected her.

He met her gaze in the mirror once again. "Please be safe."

"I'll try." She swallowed.

Emotion waged within his features as his eyes slid to her neckline. "The wire in place?"

Her pulse quickened and all she could do was nod.

His gaze returned to her face, lingering for a second longer before he turned and left.

Taking in a needy breath, she stared after him.

At times she sensed his mind and heart were untouchable. But moments like these turned the hope of them into unquenchable flames.

*****

Brice nodded his thank-you to the waitress and leaned back in the booth, his weapon pressed against his side. Steam rose from his coffee as he ran his nail across the chipped handle, his second cup this week while casing the place. This dim diner with its greasy floors and half-wilted Christmas tree left a lot to be desired, but this was the break they needed to discover the girls' location. Atlanta was big, hotels many.

He glanced at his watch, then took a sip of his coffee, making a mental note of each person in the room. The couple he'd noticed when he first walked in were now looking toward the door like he, and they weren't with the agency but with Prince. He set his mug on the epoxy-coated table and began his countdown.

Three. Two. One. Madi entered with Agent Scott on her heels.

Brice swallowed hard at the sight of them together. He hated that he wasn't the one at her side tonight. He was her bodyguard. But his job also included securing the perimeter and determining who the players were. Too much rode on this meeting, and Madi was in the center of it all.

Agent Scott led her to a table in a dark corner within view, just as they planned.

The waitress who had served him sauntered over to their table and withdrew a notebook and pen from her apron pocket. "What can I get you?" Thankfully, Brice could still hear Madi despite the fifteen-foot distance between their tables.

"Two coffees. Black?" Madi looked to Scott, and with his nod, the waitress left.

Scott leaned close and whispered something meant only for Madi. Her penetrating blue eyes narrowed in disgust. He winked.

Brice gritted his teeth.

Scott's attitude had been too relaxed and unprofessional of late, and he was on thin ice in the agency. Surely he wasn't hitting on her again? Any minute their contact would walk right through the door. What was the man thinking?

At least Brice had insisted on Madi wearing a wire. Scott knew nothing about that last-minute change, so whatever he said, Madi wasn't the only one who heard. Adam, his superior, was only a word away.

The door opened again, and their contact, Prince, walked in. A man flanked each of his sides. He smiled at Brice, arms extended. "Covington, why so far away? You're not taking your normal place next to our Constance?"

Prince never saw Madi without her bodyguard by her side, a job Brice would die for.

Brice held his gaze. "With you adding new players every time we meet, I have to stay on my game."

Prince's smile lifted one side of his mouth as he turned and ambled over to where Madi now stood. His gaze roamed every curve of her tight dress, sickening Brice's stomach. They greeted each other with a kiss to both cheeks. "So, I hear you want to help me with my shipment coming into the airport."

"You need a new location. My demand has grown. I thought we could barter." A coy smile played on her lips. "We've worked well together in the past."

"Yes. Yes, we have." His greedy eyes sparkled. "You wouldn't be a part of the deal, would you?"

Instinct brought Brice to his feet. His chest tightened.

Prince dipped his head in a slow nod toward him. "It seems Covington says no, but this one here,"—he shifted his gaze to Agent Scott, sure and steady—"he didn't even flinch. I don't trust him, and neither should you."

"Some days, I don't. Let's speak in private then."

"No need. Just dispose of him. Promise me, and I'll

reward you."

Madi leaned into Prince, and it took everything in Brice's power to hold himself where he stood. She looked into his eyes. "I like surprises. Do tell."

Prince ran a finger down her cheek. "Constance, you are hard to disappoint. I have a group coming in that haven't been branded yet. A sample, if you will."

Brice fought the anger building within him as they continued with their private discussion. Drop-off location and payment were always part of the deal, but Madi was not. The need to use this scum as a punching bag lit a fire in him that he could barely contain. But if they could rescue one child, so be it. Maybe this one child could open the door to many.

After the details had been agreed upon, Prince left with his entourage and the couple in the diner followed them out. Brice held Madi and Scott back and waited for several seconds. As he led Madi to Scott's car, his gut told him to take her with him, but he pushed the thought aside. The meeting had taken a little longer than expected, and it was almost midnight. They were supposed to be back in Winston-Salem within the hour.

Brice stopped by the passenger-side door and whispered, "Are you all right? Everything went all right with Prince?"

Madi met his gaze. "We did it," she whispered back, her eyes filling with tears. "We're going to save these girls."

"We are." He gently squeezed her arm, and she covered his hand with hers.

She smiled. "See you soon."

His breath caught and he nodded, opening the door for her. Once she'd fastened her seatbelt, he ducked his head into the vehicle to look at Scott. "I'll be behind you.

If anything out of the ordinary happens, call."

"Will do." Scott started the engine and looked to Madi, but she hadn't noticed his eyes were on her.

Brice pushed away from the car and slammed the door harder than he meant to, deciding to speak with Adam about Agent Scott's behavior toward Madi. Hopefully she wouldn't be angry at him.

He had no right to speak on her behalf when two weeks ago he had slammed a proverbial door on Madi after she'd asked him to accompany her to her brother's wedding. They had been working side by side for so long that it wasn't an unusual request, but it meant more to him. She meant more.

Brice crossed the empty parking lot and got into his black SUV. Scott had already pulled out of the lot, so Brice hurried to follow, trying to rein in his thoughts, a chore more difficult tonight than usual.

It was those days, deep undercover when he and Madi rarely spent time apart, that he got to know the real Madi. The beauty was passionate about life and loyal to those she loved, and her heart for others tugged at his soul. Like tonight, seeing the tears in her eyes for children she would never know. Sometimes he didn't think he had a soul, but the Lord, and now Madi, reminded him he did.

Brice shook his head. With three tours under his belt, he'd seen plenty of horror during both peacetime and war. He didn't need a relationship when all he had to offer was sleepless nights and memories he couldn't shake.

Too bad his mind hadn't sent his heart the memo.

Agent Scott's car swerved off the edge of the road, then darted back. Brice's grip tightened on the steering wheel, and his pulse increased as the car straightened out. He pressed the button on the steering wheel and called

Madi. No answer.

Adrenaline rushed his veins. He should have listened to his gut. It was never wrong.

As he dialed again, his phone rang. It wasn't Madi, but a number he knew well. "Adam. What's going on? Madi's with Scott."

"He discovered Madi's wire."

"There's only one way he would've discovered her wire. She didn't tell him, did she?"

"He said a few things before he realized others were listening. You need to get to her. This just turned into a hostage situation."

Adam's words faded, and the pounding in Brice's ears settled into the silence of his vehicle. His mind cleared and he knew what needed to be done. His vision focused on the car ahead. Scott's vehicle swerved across three lanes, then darted to the Interstate 85 ramp. "I'm driving toward Atlanta."

"We need this to go down quietly."

Brice ended the call and sped up so he was inches from Scott's vehicle, tailing him. At least the interstate was well lit. He didn't know how this was going to end, but quietly was the last thing on his mind. With the push of a button, he dialed Scott.

"You're not taking me in," Scott answered.

"I want Madi."

"You'll have to wait in line."

"If you hurt her—"

He gave an arrogant laugh. "You'll what? Kill me? You wouldn't be the first to try. Besides, Madi's with me now."

Disdain tainted Brice's tongue. "What have you done to her?"

Scott began to whistle. Seconds ticked by as a slow

burn snaked its way through Brice's core before the man finally answered. "So, you want to know my secret? We all know how Madi likes bottled water when she returns to the car."

He'd kill him. "What did you give her?"

"She won't remember. Besides, I'm good at what I do, playing both sides. Can you imagine what my partners will say when they find out she's an agent and I hand her over to them on a platter. I think they'll have a little fun with her, don't you?"

Brice gripped the steering wheel. "Scott, let me tell you how this is going down. The agency wants it quiet, but I don't care if it makes the front page. You have one choice. Release Madi or your family will find you in the morgue. Because if you think I'm going to let you drive off with her, you don't know me at all. She has a better chance of survival if I crash your car into the concrete guardrail."

Scott went silent, and Brice glanced at the screen to make sure the call hadn't ended.

"Your tactics don't scare me."

Stepping on the gas, Brice rammed his SUV into Scott's bumper, jerking them across two lanes.

Scott swore and caught control of his vehicle. "Back off!" His breathing came out ragged, desperate. He sped up, swerving in front of a truck, and almost hit another vehicle.

Nearing one hundred miles per hour, Brice followed at a short distance. Two semi-trucks were ahead side by side and he had a plan and he prayed it worked. He closed in again and rode Scott's bumper, pushing him toward the semis.

"Stop! I want a trade! Car for car. I'll take yours. You take mine. Madi included. Before you kill us!"

"Where?" Brice eased off the accelerator and glanced at his odometer. Scott's speed was increasing as he drove past the semis on the shoulder. He followed.

"Here. On the interstate. Out of view. Leave the car running."

Scott ended the call, and his speed began to taper, the semis passing them both. Once they were out of view of the interstate surveillance cameras, they slowed to the side of the road, Brice nearing Scott's bumper.

Brice removed his Sig from a hidden compartment and gave Scott time to make his move. He had been careless and impatient lately, and Brice anticipated the man was either going to drive off or come after him.

Scott finally eased his door open, gun drawn.

Brice opened the driver-side door and ducked behind it. "Scott, this isn't going to end like you think it will!"

"I know all about you. I've heard the stories. You come back from war on your high horse. You're nothing here, Brice. I'm about to take you down."

He'd once been stuck in a building with the Taliban, shots buzzing by his head. In those moments of life and death and war, there was nothing but silence as he zoned in on the enemy. Regardless of the target. "And you think you, one guy with a gun, affects me in the slightest?"

Scott fired. A crack sounded and shards of glass fell to Brice's feet.

Taking a step from the SUV, Brice aimed at the heart.

CHAPTER TWO

"Madi. Can you hear me?" Brice turned off the car and leaned across the console, gently palming Madi's cheek. She turned her face into his hand, and he felt the full impact of the moment. A slight moan left her throat. Her eyes had yet to open.

It didn't matter what he said. She wouldn't recall a word of it tomorrow. Yet the need to apologize pushed him the last four hours as he drove to her home near Helen, Georgia.

"Scott drugged you, babe. I'm so sorry. It's my fault. *My* fault. If I'd listened to my gut, that pig wouldn't have—" He growled, reaching over her and opening her door. After walking around to the passenger side, he lifted her out of the car and held her to his chest. She snuggled against him, and his heart ached.

And to think he'd almost lost her...

He swallowed the bile climbing his throat.

He was tempted to hold her until she shook off this drug-induced fog—to allow the proof she was safe and alive to sink in—but he knew better. The feel of her now was too much.

After entering her home, Brice found her bedroom, tucked her under the covers, and closed the door behind him. He took a heavy breath and pushed himself outside to the car, collecting their suitcases. After scanning the perimeter of her house, he reentered and bolted the lock.

Brice glanced around Madi's house. The next several weeks would stretch him possibly more than he could bear. Madi was his new asset, and he was to protect her at all cost.

How was he going to accomplish this objective without falling hard for her?

Over the last year he'd fought to keep himself in check and control his feelings, but slowly he was losing the battle. He knew it was coming, like a storm, raging in the horizon.

He would ruin them. PTSD had a way of capturing a mind and torturing a soul.

It was only a matter of time.

****

Madi's eyes opened before closing again. She stretched out across the bed then turned onto her side. A breeze from above floated down around her. She smiled, enjoying being in her own bed.

At the thought, she blinked her eyes open. She was home.

She jerked upright and glanced around. Everything was the way she'd left it almost nine months ago. A hairband even still teetered on the edge of her dresser. The same one she'd hunted for on her drive back to her apartment in North Carolina.

Was she dreaming? She looked to the door. Was that

coffee she smelled?

She pulled down the covers and planted her feet on the floor. She was dressed in neon pink and green pajamas her sister Rachel had brought back from Florida. A set Madi took with her to North Carolina and washed but couldn't bring herself to wear. It was obnoxious and glowed in the dark.

Madi exited her bedroom to find Brice leaning against the back door, a mug in hand. She slowed her steps as she neared, taking in the sight of him, how his broad shoulders pulled at his navy blue T-shirt and how his dark hair touched the tops of his ears. A bit longer than he liked.

His gaze pointed toward the wooded backyard, but she was certain he sensed her presence. He had an uncanny way of knowing when she was near. It was eerie at times, but at other times she wanted to believe it was because of their connection to each other.

"Nice pajamas." He took a sip from his mug, but kept his gaze through the window.

She crossed her arms against her chest, pretending his words or the butterflies in her stomach didn't exist. "What are we doing here, Brice? And how do you even know about this place? I've never mentioned it."

"You did. On the way here. Told me where the key was hidden." He turned and nodded at the couch. "Sit with me."

"Nothing makes sense."

He neared, placing a hand on her back.

She didn't move, couldn't move.

"Please," he whispered close to her ear.

Madi inhaled a slow breath and forced her feet to obey.

He set his cup on the coffee table before sitting

alongside her.

"Why am I wearing pajamas I can't stand? And why can't I seem to remember putting them on?"

"What do you recall about yesterday?"

She glanced down at her lap and folded her hands. "I'm not sure. The last thing I remember is being with Scott in the car."

"Is that all?" Brice's expression hardened. Emotions she couldn't identify flashed across his eyes. He stood.

She studied him as he paced, the tightening of his jaw. "What happened that you're not telling me?"

"My gut told me to take you with me after our meeting with Prince, but it had gone longer than expected, and … it's my fault." He paused his pacing and frowned. "Scott slipped a date rape drug called GHB in the bottled water you had in his car. I hadn't caught on when he sped away from the diner parking lot, leaving me rushing to catch up. It seems the two of you had some type of struggle in the vehicle while he was driving."

Madi stood. "Wait. Scott drugged me?"

"Yes." Brice's lips flattened into a firm line, his forehead creased. "From what Adam mentioned, you were still conscious at the time but already going under."

A memory hovered in her mind.

Brice ran his fingers through his hair. "I had no idea what was going on until his car swerved—"

"He attacked me." She looked at Brice, the words bitter on her tongue. "I remember. I was trying to fight him off, but I felt so weak. That's when he found my wire." As the truth sank in, her hands began to shake.

Brice took several steps to her. "Let's sit down."

She met his gaze, and a tightness grew in her chest. "Where's Scott now? Looking for me?"

"No, the agency has him."

"Then why are we here?" The memories of Scott's hands on her, his words assaulting her, brought apprehension even now.

"Madi, you're shaking."

The desire to fall into Brice's arms for comfort, for protection, silenced her. She needed him and his strength, but he'd been distancing himself from her for weeks. She couldn't stand for him to push her away now.

Madi moved from his closeness, her heart tearing with each step. She wrapped her arms around her middle and stared blindly out the window where Brice had stood earlier.

He came and stood behind her. "I know this isn't how you envisioned everything playing out. What happened with Scott—"

"There's nothing I can do about it. I only hope I can continue as Constance. Too many lives are at stake."

"Yours included."

She glanced over her shoulder at him. "I'm safe now." A hard shiver ran through her and she turned her gaze to a bluebird in the yard as it hopped across the grass. "Please tell me you didn't dress me in these hideous pajamas."

"At the time, I was packing your things from your apartment. The drugs had kicked in, and you were in a drunk-like state. You came up behind me and said you were going to change. Ten minutes later you found me and had a smile on your face. I thought you liked them."

She could only imagine why she was smiling, probably gawking at him. Hopefully she hadn't made a fool of herself. "Rachel bought them for me when she and her family went to Florida about nine months back. I couldn't bring myself to wear them, I guess, until now."

"You look like you belong on a tropical island

somewhere."

She gave him a half smile. He was trying to make her feel better. That had to count for something. "Thank you."

"So, when is your brother's wedding?"

"In less than a week. I told my family I'd be here to help out with any last minute details." She shrugged. "I'm early." Something caught her eye near one of the bar stools. She strolled over to where two suitcases stood. "Are these yours?"

"They are. I decided to take you up on your invitation to join you for your brother's wedding."

"I never meant…" How could she fix this? "I'm sorry, Brice, but you can't stay here."

He grinned roguishly. "Why not?"

He was playing with her now. "You know why. We can't stay under the same roof night after night. Once my family knows I'm here, they'll come over. My brother. What would he say?"

His grin vanished. "In all seriousness, I guess I don't see the issue. We've been under the same roof before. Many nights."

He was right, and they both knew it.

Nevertheless, hearing the words come from his mouth warmed her cheeks. "But that was work, surveillance. We were undercover. This is different. This is my house. My family. When I asked you to come to the wedding with me, I never planned on you staying here. My brother-in-law's parents have a hotel in Helen."

"I see."

She looked to her hands. "I only thought a trip together that wasn't about work would be nice. For us to be *real* together. For once. Like normal people."

His brows furrowed as his eyes darted to his luggage.

"I'm afraid that's not going to happen now."

"What do you mean?"

"Let's sit back down. There are some things I need to share with you."

She hesitated for a moment, but seeing the corners of his mouth tilt into a frown, she did as he had asked.

Brice sat, turning toward her. "After what happened with Scott..." His jaw clenched again, and as if a storm was brewing in his gaze, his blue eyes darkened. "I just started driving. Adam called, and we discussed where to take you. Someplace for you to fly under the radar for a while. I told him about your brother's wedding. He remembered and gave me a new assignment, and then one for both of us."

"What kind of assignments?"

"After your brother's wedding, we're going to Vienna. Observation only, but they need an extra pair of eyes and ears."

"That's not too bad. Easy really."

"There's a catch, Madi. We're to be married. Our names are Mr. and Mrs. Shafer, visiting from the States. While we're here for your brother's wedding, they want us practicing the role."

She was stunned into silence. All this time she'd been good at hiding her feelings from Brice, and now the agency was asking her to throw all that away. "I can't."

"Madi—"

"I can't pretend to be in love with you." Her heart seized within her chest, stealing her breath. She started to stand, but Brice covered her hand on her knee with his, halting her.

"There's more." The timber of his voice was calm, strong, something she struggled to feel.

Perhaps Brice could sense her continued withdrawal

from him, her need to escape the conversation, because his palm tightened on hers.

"The agency is trying to contain the situation with Scott, but if they can't, this puts you in danger. They might hang Scott out to dry and use him as cover for us. If that happens, they'll take Prince down and hopefully uncover the girls."

"Is that why they sent us here, into hiding?"

"Yes. And the other assignment, Madi, is for me—to protect you."

She yanked her hand away from his and rose to her feet. "I need to go."

"Where?" He stood.

"Anywhere. To see my brother." She glanced around, trying to retain her bearings. Where was her purse? "I need my keys."

"Your car isn't here. I drove, remember?"

She eyed him, wishing she had remembered. "I need yours then."

"You're not leaving me, Madi. Wherever you go, I'm going."

She stiffened. "I'm going alone. And if you try to stop me, Mr. and Mrs. Shafer will be divorced faster than you can blink an eye."

"Vienna is only an assignment. Two days. It has nothing to do with us. Why are you pushing me away so hard?"

Madi almost laughed. "You've been pushing me away for weeks. Maybe it's time we put some distance between us."

Confusion flittered over his features before understanding registered in his gaze. The way he was staring at her now, her cheeks burned.

She held out her hand. "Keys."

"Where are you going?"

She inhaled a calming breath. "To my brother's. And probably to Rachel's, but she might be out with Amabelle."

"I need their addresses, and you need to change."

Madi glanced down, her hand falling to her side. Here she was making a stand, and she was still in these stinking pajamas.

Brice reached into his pocket and withdrew a set of keys. Surprisingly, without another comment, he let her take them.

****

While Madi was changing, Brice withdrew his cell from his pocket, located a cab service, and dialed.

His phone vibrated, and as he requested, Madi had sent Patrick and Rachel's contact information. He saved them to his phone, and upon hearing a friendly greeting on the line, he glanced toward Madi's bedroom door.

"Yes, I need a cab, and I'm not sure for how long. I have a few stops to make."

CHAPTER THREE

Madi inhaled a long breath as she stood on Patrick's doorstep. After her conversation with Brice, she wasn't ready to see her brother, but she had to get it over with. Brice's assignment would force him to stay by her side, and she couldn't allow Patrick to come over and see her and Brice together without warning.

Her brother's opinion of her was the only one that mattered. He loved her unconditionally, and was the only one who could see through her pretenses or sense how much people and life affected her. Over the years Patrick had been her strength and her home at times, and when she'd decided what she wanted to do with her life, he'd supported her in every way.

Madi knocked, paused, and then rang the doorbell three times like they used to do when they were children. His secret code was slightly different. Would he recall hers?

The door flung open, and Patrick's beaming smile met her. "You're here." But much too soon his handsome smile faded. His blue eyes, so much like hers, held concern. "Early. You're never early. Is everything all right?"

Emotion clogged her throat. She took a step inside, and he clasped her in a hug.

"Whatever it is, you're home," he whispered against her hair.

"I am."

He moved her to arm's length and closed the door behind them. "Where are you staying?"

"At the house." She palmed his clean shaven cheek. "I'm not used to this look."

"I painted the house and splattered it on my hands. I had an itch." He shrugged. "Couldn't get married with paint on my beard." He ran a hand over his jaw with a faraway look in his eye. His smile returned. "It'll grow back in time for the wedding."

He was such a devoted brother and soon-to-be husband and father. What a precious gift. Would the Lord ever allow her to find such a man? "Amabelle is blessed to have you."

"And I, her." He seemed to glow as he led them into the kitchen. "Had your coffee yet?"

"No. Is it that obvious?"

"Slightly. Coffee helps you relax. Which will help with my interrogation."

Madi chuckled. "You know my weakness." She dropped her purse on a bar stool and strolled the open floor plan. He'd put a lot of work into the house since she was last here. "The place looks great."

Patrick opened a fresh bag of coffee beans and poured them into the grinder. "Amabelle and I watched quite a few home-improvement shows, and it looked easy, so I went with it."

"Removing a few of the walls worked out nicely. It

makes the place seem larger than Rachel's." She took two coffee mugs from the cabinet and set them on the counter while Patrick ground and started the coffee. "So, how's the family doing?"

"Rachel's doing well. Tim's been traveling more for work, so it's been good for Rachel to keep busy with the wedding preparations. The boys are growing like weeds." He poured coffee into their mugs. "And how are you?"

She gave him a sideways glance. "For the first time in my life, I'm not sure."

Patrick handed her a mug, and she followed him to the breakfast nook that looked out over the wooded backyard. "Want to tell me about it?"

"I'm not sure where to begin, and it's entwined tightly with work,"—she glanced down at her mug—"but it has to do with the man I was telling you about."

"Brice?"

She could sense Patrick's gaze on her. "Yes. And he's here with me. Waiting for me at the house. We're on assignment."

"The reason you're early." He took a sip of his coffee. She could see the wheels in her brother's mind working. "Are you okay with this assignment?"

"No. Not exactly."

"Because of your feelings for him?"

"The lines between work and my personal life are about to cross. Brice will be staying with me at the house, and I have no say-so in the matter." Madi glanced away. She bit back a comment, recalling how Brice looked when she walked out of the house with his keys. "Maybe if it were on my terms ... it would be easier."

"Then why not turn the situation into your terms? You care about Brice. He's here with you for the wedding as you wanted, though I prefer he stay at a hotel. Perhaps your time with him will show you if he's the right one to build a relationship with."

She lifted her mug to her lips and savored the dark brew. Inhaling the aroma, she knew he was right. She was looking at her situation and not allowing God to show her the direction she should go. The Lord had never failed her, and He definitely wouldn't start now. "I think you're right. I can make this work."

"Good, because I've never known you to throw in the towel so easily."

Madi studied her coffee cup before meeting his eyes. "It's been a hard two days."

His expression dulled, and he covered her hands with his own. "Your strained expression says there's a lot you're not telling me, but never forget the Lord is near, and I'm here too."

Madi leaned over and kissed his cheek. "Why do you think I came?"

****

Brice quickly punched the On button to the Keurig and waited for the water to warm. Thankfully the cab driver took a short cut to the house and Madi was right behind him.

Placing the mug into the machine, he waited for his coffee. Madi knew he'd been pushing her away, but did she understand why?

That was the question he'd continued to ask himself as he watched and waited for her at every stop she made. Madi was also an agent and now his asset. She should have been nothing more to him.

"But she meant a great deal more."

He was the one who put distance between them. He

was the one who controlled how much time they spent together outside of work. Letting himself get too close, too involved was a mistake.

But her words "time apart" didn't settle well.

Taking a sip from his mug, he carried his coffee to the front wraparound porch and lowered into a brown rocker. She should be driving up any minute.

The snap of a twig sat him up straighter, his firearm against his body calling to him. Ears attentive, he scanned the perimeter. Another twig snapped to his right. He set the mug down and slowly stood, slipping his gun into his palm. The sounds around him drowned out, all but the one. No neighbor lived on either side of the house. Brice moved down the porch steps, then a rustling of leaves made him pause.

Craning his neck, he turned and set his target in his sights. A doe lifted her head and met his gaze for a moment before darting off.

Brice held his position for a moment longer. The tightness in his muscles coiled even more, sending a familiar sensation rippling through him.

Where was Madi?

CHAPTER FOUR

Madi pulled into her driveway, but before she had a chance to set the vehicle in park, Brice came barreling from the house. She shouldn't have been gone so long.

He wrenched open the driver's side door and loomed over her. His pure size and strength could make a person cower, but not her. His gaze bore into her, blue eyes telegraphing his thoughts. Concern, frustration.

She wanted him to say something, share how he was feeling. He hid so much of himself from her, and she desired more. To know him. To love him. If only he'd allow it.

"Hi." She exited the car, noting his clenched jaw, and went to the trunk. "I bought dinner." And several other things, but now wasn't the time to mention a few of those were his favorites. She lifted two plastic bags before Brice joined her.

"Go inside," he growled, taking the bags from her. "I've got this. You've had a long day."

She glanced at the thirty-plus bags she'd loaded into the car and seemed to wilt at the thought of hauling them in. It took little convincing with her body rebelling against her sheer will to keep going. "Thank you."

The aroma of coffee greeted her when she entered the house. She set her purse on the counter and began putting away the groceries Brice brought to her. By the time they had unloaded each sack and stuffed the plastic bags in the recycling bin, her hunger gave way to exhaustion.

"I tried to call," Brice finally said. "You didn't answer."

"I must have left my phone somewhere." She leaned against the counter and yawned, covering her mouth in time.

He stood alongside her. "Amabelle said for you to call Patrick when you got home. He wants to know you made it back all right."

"Thankfully, I decided to keep my landline. I'll call him. I don't want him to worry."

"I get concerned about you as well, Madi."

She gave him a tired smile. "I know. It's your job." Hurt showed in his eyes, and she realized too late what she'd said. Yet she was too drained to find the words to apologize. She needed a shower and her bed.

"Help yourself to anything. See you tomorrow." Madi pushed off the counter and headed toward her room.

"Good night." Brice's whispered words reached her, and her heart squeezed with sorrow. He cared about her. He made it clear time and time again, but she thought they might be more. Hoped and prayed they would.

Perhaps Brice wasn't the right one to build a relationship with. She'd been burned before. Maybe her brother was right, and she just learned a valuable lesson. One-sided love never grew.

****

Brice couldn't sleep. He had to fix this with Madi. Her words stung and his insides rolled with disgust. At himself, his inadequacies, and at the possibility he was on the verge of losing her.

A door creaked slightly, alerting him that Madi was awake. The light streaming from the kitchen must have drawn her. She walked past him, wearing a robe and flannel pants that dragged along the tops of her red-painted toes. She disappeared into the kitchen.

He cleared his throat before entering so as not to frighten her. "Can't sleep?"

Madi reached for a glass in the cabinet and filled it with water from the refrigerator door. "Not really," she said flatly.

"Me either." Brice eased over to her. "Are you hungry? You didn't eat dinner. I can fix you something."

Avoiding his gaze, she took a long drink from her glass. "I'm fine."

She wasn't fine, and for the first time since he'd known her, he pushed the Proceed with Caution signs from his mind and did what he felt. He lifted her jaw with his finger, forcing her to look at him. A shimmer of a tear still lingered beneath her lashes, but it was her wild curls, full lips, and swollen eyes that stabbed him in the chest.

He wiped the moisture with his thumb, taken aback by her once again. "I'm here for you, Madi. Not for the job, but because of you. This is where I want to be."

Madi blinked twice, then opened her mouth as if she planned to say something. Instead, she pressed her lips together and leaned into his chest.

He wrapped his arms around her and pulled her closer, fully aware of how perfectly she fit against him.

After several seconds had passed, she slid her arms around him and let out a long breath against his neck. "I can't get Scott … My mind won't sleep. I want this night to end. A new day to begin."

If there was one thing he knew well, nights were the hardest when the mind decided to play a game of concentration. The past was always included. Tonight he'd try to make a new memory for Madi, one that would champion his cause. Time apart from this woman in his arms wasn't an option.

"Come sit with me." Brice spoke against her hair, inhaling the soft scent of her flowery shampoo. She nodded, and he led her to the couch. He reached over to a worn rocking chair and slipped a quilt that hung off the arm of the chair to her lap. "Here you go." When he sat next to her, she leaned against his shoulder.

Her fingers skimmed the quilt. "I'm sorry I was gone for such a long time today. I needed to see my family, to feel grounded. Safe."

Her words pricked his pride. Did she not feel safe with him? There were only two things Brice could offer Madi, his protection and the peace of knowing he'd be there. He had been, willingly, without thought. Had he failed her so completely? "Don't I make you feel protected?"

"You do, but it's temporary, comes with the job. And then when the job is over, it's over. It's not real."

"Aren't I sitting with you? I'm real, Madi. When I'm with you, there's no pretense."

She leaned to the side and raised an eyebrow at him.

"Okay, so maybe with our job there is, but that excludes now, moments like these."

"How will I know the difference when we're to pretend to be lovers, married? I don't think I can do that with you."

"It's only two days."

"You're not following me."

"Then tell me. I'm trying to understand."

She looked to her hands. "I have feelings for you, real feelings. The kind of feelings that anticipate seeing you, being with you. I've been waiting for a sign from you that you feel the same. What happened in the kitchen confuses me. Not once have you touched me the way you did, and all I can do is wonder if you've already slipped into character."

"I see." And he did, clearly. If he had a penny for every time he thought of calling her just to hear her voice, texting to make sure she was safe, holding her or her hand, pressing a kiss against her full lips, he'd be putting in for retirement.

Brice reached over and cupped her hand in her lap, entwining their fingers. He had to prove to Madi he wasn't the type of guy who would toy with her feelings. What he did and said, he meant, wholeheartedly. "Then let me assure you, the way I touched you in the kitchen— now or in the future—has nothing to do with playing a part. It has everything to do with my feelings for you. Seeing you moments ago and knowing what you endured today, I couldn't help myself. I wanted to comfort you. Had to comfort you and make sure you know I'm here."

She leaned her head on his shoulder again. "What does this mean for us?"

"I'm not sure, but I don't want time apart from you. It might not be the answer you're wanting or …"

"It's enough for me." She snuggled closer and tugged on the quilt. Brice brought her to his chest, astounded by the turn of events, thankful nevertheless.

It wasn't long before her breathing evened out and his own eyes grew heavy. He'd never been as content as he was now holding Madi. Perhaps he was kidding himself, already playing the role of her lover. Reality would find him soon enough, as would the images of war he continued to fight long after the battle had been won.

CHAPTER FIVE

"Brrr! It's cold! Aren't you cold?" Madi rubbed her arms against a shiver and slammed the car door shut with her gloved hand.

Brice chuckled. "I'm from the North, remember. This is summer." He placed a hand on her back, and she shivered again, unsure if it was from the cold or his touch.

He led her to Amabelle's pet store, and Madi paused at the door though she'd rather plow into the heated building. "Thanks again for agreeing to help with the store and Abby. I know this isn't what you expected to be doing, but after talking with my brother, I wanted to help out any way I could."

"You're welcome." He slid a strand of hair from her face, grazing her cheek in the process. "Now go inside before you freeze." He opened the door, and the bell chimed overhead.

"Be right with you," Amabelle's voice sang as she neared. Her brown eyes widened upon seeing Madi. "Patrick didn't tell me you were in town!"

Madi clasped her closest friend and soon-to-be sister-in-law in a hug. "I told him I wanted to surprise you."

"You did." She held her a moment longer, then looked to Brice, brow arching. "And who do we have here?"

Instantly, Madi felt the rise of a blush and reprimanded herself for it. She couldn't go around blushing all over the place when she introduced him. "Amabelle, this is my friend, Brice."

Amabelle held out her hand, and Brice accepted. "Nice to meet you," they said in unison, and Amabelle smiled, sneaking a peek at Madi.

Madi had no idea what Amabelle was thinking, but now wasn't the time to find out. "We came to help," she said quickly. "Patrick had mentioned you're a little overwhelmed with freight and wedding details, so we thought we'd chip in. What do you say?"

Amabelle grabbed Madi in another hug, then pushed her to arm's length. "Are you kidding? Because if you're not, I accept. I need to go to Atlanta. My wedding dress is ready to be picked up, and I haven't been able to go."

"We're at your service," Brice stated, his handsome grin spreading to Madi's heart.

Amabelle clapped her hands in front of her. "Can you start now? Abby has just fallen asleep, and with her walking all over the place, she wears herself out. Her naps usually last about two hours. I can be back by the time she wakes up."

"We'd love to." Madi slipped off her jacket and removed her gloves, setting them on the counter near the register. "What would you have us do?"

"The new merchandise in the back would be a big help." Amabelle grabbed her cell from her back pocket. "Abby has everything she needs in her bag—from diapers and food, to extra sets of clothes. I'll call Patrick and let him know of our plans." She tucked her brown hair behind one ear and hurried off to the back of the store.

A moment later, Amabelle returned holding her cell between her ear and shoulder, slipping her purse strap across her body. "Yes, Madi and Brice are here. They'll keep Abby. She's just fallen asleep." She kissed Madi's cheek before heading out.

Madi looked to Brice. "Ready to work?"

"Lead the way."

Just as Amabelle had predicted, two hours later Abby's tiny voice sounded from her mother's office. Madi carried the last box of flea and tick collars, adding it to the stack of inventory. "What more do we have left to do?"

Brice shrink-wrapped the previous pallet they had finished. "Home and yard sprays, plus a few leashes we must have set aside and forgotten about."

Madi placed the scanner down and stretched out her back. "I need to wash up before getting Abby. I can finish this later."

"I got this." He winked and grabbed ahold of the pallet jack. "Go, so I can concentrate."

Madi caught sight of his smile, but it was Abby's sorrowful cry that pulled her attention away. When she entered Amabelle's office, Abby was standing in the play yard. Tears ran down her face.

"Oh, sweetie, come here." She reached for her, and the precious little girl held out her arms.

Abby lowered her head on Madi's neck and pointed in no particular direction. "Ma-ma?"

"Mommy will be here in just a little bit." Feeling her saggy bloomers, Madi lifted the diaper bag and carried it over to a couch Amabelle had purchased several years ago when she first opened the pet store. Memories of their shopping expedition brought a smile to her face. They had been friends since they were children, and to think her brother and dearest friend were finally getting married after all this time still amazed her. It hadn't been an easy road for them when they traveled down different paths, but Madi believed in soulmates, and Patrick and Amabelle were exactly that.

Could Brice be hers?

After changing Abby's diaper, Madi fished through the bag and found several containers of applesauce, a microwaveable cup of mac and cheese, diced veggies and fruit in small colored containers. Abby's eyes brightened, and she began clapping her hands, causing Madi to chuckle, "I knew you'd be hungry. Let's sit you in your highchair, and I'll feed you."

****

Brice's pulse raced at the sight of Madi. She set two containers, one sliced pears and the other oranges, on the high chair, then added water to the mac and cheese before placing it in the microwave. She turned around and swooped Abby within her arms and began kissing her chubby cheeks.

Abby squirmed, and the sweetest little giggles filled his ears.

He was intruding on their moment, but he couldn't pull himself away. Madi's smile. The way she and Abby laughed. He'd seen Madi many ways, from an undercover beauty who demanded attention, to a Sig-carrying tough law enforcement officer with a marksmanship many wished they possessed, but this, with Abby...

He took a step, and a dull ache seized him. Madi made him want a life he'd once desired, a family to call his own. A dream swallowed by war and a hidden truth—he wasn't the man he once was.

Madi didn't seem to care though. She'd had a glimpse into his world. They never talked about the night she sat with him while they watched the sunrise, or how being near her brought an unexplainable peace.

He would never tell her how deeply he'd needed her that night or the nights afterward when he prayed for God's peace and thought of her. He would never tell her how she made him question his sanity at keeping her at a distance.

Maybe he did leave his sanity behind in the tunnels of Afghanistan, or when an IED hit his unit in Iraq and he'd walked away with only a metal fragment while his friends were dismembered.

Madi's prayer of grace caught his attention, and Abby babbled right along.

He yanked his gaze away and retreated into the pet store. The memories of the past grew, and he hardened his heart to the ache within.

He didn't deserve Madi, and he knew it.

CHAPTER SIX

Propping Abby on her hip, Madi grabbed the fish food and sprinkled several pieces into the tanks.

Abby leaned forward and pressed her small fingers against the glass. "Ishy."

Madi pointed to one of the guppies. "Aren't they pretty? See its tail?" The bell above the door rang and before she moved a step, Brice had come from the back room and joined her. "Do you want to hold Abby?"

He glanced down at Abby for a split second then back at the door. "Let me check it out."

"Amabelle," a man called, and Brice held out his hand for Madi to wait. Abby didn't seem to care what Brice was saying because she began to rock and swing her feet as if to say, *let's go.*

Brice ambled down the aisle and disappeared behind the critter carriers. "Can I help you?" his voice strong, unsalesman like.

The man asked for Amabelle or Patrick. There was something familiar about his voice, so Madi made her way to the front of the store and smiled at Amabelle's older brother. "Asher."

His eyes widened. "Madilyn, you never returned my text. I'm glad you're here." He bent and kissed her cheek.

Madi felt Brice's gaze on her. "How are you?"

"Doing well. If you haven't heard, I made partner."

She hadn't. "Congratulations. I know it's always been your dream."

"One of many," Asher gave her a deliberate grin, one she and Brice wouldn't miss.

Heat rose to Madi's neck, and she sensed Brice's unwavering presence. "Asher, I'd like for you to meet my friend, Brice Johnson, and you know your sweet niece." Madi focused on Abby instead of the man who'd carried a torch for her since high school or the man who twisted her middle into knots.

Asher smiled at Brice. "Nice to meet you. A friend of Madilyn's is a friend of mine." He reached for Abby, and the little girl giggled her way into his arms. "Abby girl, you've grown since February."

Madi frowned. "You were here in February?"

He eyed her with a reassuring glance. "I was coming to see you. It seems we missed each other by two days."

Brice cleared his throat. "Amabelle should be back after a while. We'll let her know you stopped by."

Was Brice standing taller, wider? All she could think of was the turkeys her family raised and how the more dominant male would drop his wings and fan out his feathers.

Brice was strutting!

Madi bit back a smile. She wanted to wrap her arms around Brice and kiss him senseless. "Asher, where are you staying?"

He pulled his gaze from Brice and looked to Abby. "At the hotel. We're to have dinner tonight at Patrick's."

He kissed the top of Abby's head and passed her back to Madi. "I had hoped you'd be there. I'd like to catch up."

"I'm not sure what our plans are, but I'll let Amabelle know if we can make it."

Asher gave her a half smile. Regret lingered in his gaze. "Bye, Madilyn." He gave a tight nod to Brice then headed out the door.

She wasn't sure if she should mention Brice's behavior toward Asher or just let it go, but when Brice went to the front of the store, locked the door, and turned the open sign to Closed, all she could do was gape. "It's not even one o'clock yet. We still have a little over four hours."

"It's closing time." He walked past her, opened the register, and withdrew his wallet. He stuffed several bills into the till.

"What are you doing?"

"I'm paying Amabelle for the time she's closed." He shut the register. "Anyone can walk in here."

Madi thought for a moment and glanced at the door. "Asher's driven, but he's not a threat if that's what you're referring to. I've known him for years."

His jaw clinched, and he met her gaze in a challenge.

Her phone rang, and she slipped it from her front pocket, setting Abby on her feet. Patrick's number shone on screen. "Hey."

"Listen, sis, I'm on my way to Atlanta. Amabelle's car broke down."

"Is she all right?"

"Fine. Frustrated. Can you do us a favor and keep Abby? I'm not sure what time we'll be back."

Madi looked up in time to see Abby run down the aisle. She hurried after her. "Of course. No problem. Abby can come back with me and stay the night. Amabelle packed enough stuff for a week."

"You don't mind? I know Rachel could, but with Tim gone, she already has her hands full."

Madi couldn't imagine watching more than one child at a time, especially one who just learned her feet could take her places. "Abby will be fine. Now go rescue your damsel in distress." Panting, she headed down the fish aisle. Abby halted then pointed at the aquarium.

"Thanks. And while I've got you, can you call Asher? He phoned, but I didn't pick up in time. We were to have dinner tonight."

She lifted Abby and showed her the fish. "Sure, I've got his number at the house. I'll call when I get home. Now be safe."

"You were chasing her, weren't you?"

"Abby will keep me fit for sure."

He chuckled. "Glad you're home. See you soon."

Madi palmed her cell and slid it back into her pocket. She switched Abby to her other hip and scanned the store. From where she stood, Brice couldn't be found to continue their conversation. Perhaps it was for the best. There would be plenty of time later.

A noise sounded. Brice hauled a pallet across the floor, and her eyes drifted to his tribal tattoo peeking out from beneath his sleeve. He stopped at the end of several aisles.

"Come on, Abby girl. Let's see what he's up to." Madi set Abby down and held her hand as they walked over to where Brice was carrying merchandise off the pallet. "It seems you've done this before."

He shrugged. "I worked at a mom and pop store back in school for a few years after football season was over. The man's son and I basically ran the place, so I'm pretty familiar with the ins and outs." He carried several boxes to an end cap and began refilling the pegs. "Might as well get these things on the floor since we're closed."

Madi led Abby to a box of dog collars and gave her two to hold. She tried to add them to the bottom pegs while Madi added them to the top. "You're a big helper. I know your mommy is so proud of you."

Madi looked to Brice. "My brother called. Said Amabelle's car broke down on the way back from Atlanta. I told him I'd keep Abby overnight and call Asher to let him know dinner is off."

She picked up another stack of collars and thought about Asher. If Brice hadn't been here, she'd have invited him over or to go out to eat. She saw Asher as nothing more than a friend, regardless of his hints over the years. Besides, they were to be family soon. Didn't that mean some type of invitation was in order since he really didn't know anyone else in town?

"Is Amabelle all right?"

Of course he'd ask. He was that type of guy, and she loved him for it.

Love.

Her pulse rose. Had she fallen in love with him?

He pinned her with a gaze. "Madi, is Patrick's fiancée all right?"

She looked up at him, hearing the concern in his voice. "She's fine. More frustrated than anything else." She glanced around for Abby, taking the collars she'd slid onto the wrong pegs and adding them to the correct ones.

"Abby grabbed a few of the cat toys at the end cap over there and plopped down."

She followed his nod. The little girl was now lying on her back, holding a fake mouse by the tail over her head. "I think when I call Asher, we should invite him out or over for dinner. I feel bad for him not knowing anyone in town when he was to have supper with my brother and his sister."

He glanced away. "Whatever you'd like to do."

"Okay." Madi walked back to the pallet suddenly confused. She'd expected a protest. Hadn't Brice closed the store because of Asher? Hadn't he been acting like he couldn't stand the man, or had she misread him earlier?

She hoped tonight wasn't a mistake.

CHAPTER SEVEN

Brice rubbed the back of his neck and tried to talk himself down from one of the biggest mistakes he'd ever made.

Asher was to arrive at any minute. A man who obviously took a great deal of interest in Madi. Brice's gut burned as he recalled the way Asher had looked at her.

You're an idiot for agreeing.

The doorbell rang, and he left his room for the door, but Madi had beat him to it. He had yet to catch a glimpse of her since she'd showered and put Abby down for the night. She wore her favorite pair of jeans, a T-shirt she'd bought at a flea market when they were passing through the Midwest, and no shoes or socks.

She wasn't trying to impress anyone.

Asher was a different story in his sports jacket, khakis, and an expectant smile as he handed her a large bouquet of small flowers.

She pressed the flowers to her chest and inhaled. "Ranunculus aren't in season until next month. How did you find them?"

"My secret."

"My favorite."

"I remember." His grin grew.

She inhaled her bouquet again. "Please, come in. Let me find a vase for these."

Asher closed the door behind him, and while leaving his shoes in the foyer, he caught Brice watching. His brows furrowed. "I didn't realize you'd be here."

Did he plan on staying a while?

"Madi didn't tell you?" Brice strolled to him and held out his hand.

Asher hesitated for a moment, then shook with a firm grip. "No. Perhaps she forgot." He shoved his hands in his pockets. "I didn't see you at the family's hotel."

"I'm staying with Madi. She's very thoughtful."

Asher glanced around. "You can say that."

Madi joined them. "Say what?"

Brice wanted to say how breathtaking she was and how much he'd enjoyed being at the flea market with her. The way they were together, the way she laughed… Things he should have said before now. "Excuse me, let me check on Abby. Is she in your room?"

"She is, but…" Madi looked from Brice to Asher. "Give us a minute. We'll be right back." She led him to her room and gently closed the door. A light shone from the bathroom. "You're tense," she whispered, and Abby squirmed under the covers. Madi drew close, touching his arm. "Is he the reason you closed the store early?"

Brice leaned to her ear. "If you must know. Yes."

She looked up, her cheek grazing his. Her palm tightened against his arm. He was tempted to lean in and claim a kiss but held himself in place. She hid her face from him and dropped her hand. "You should have said something."

"Sometimes people forget to mention things, because they're in a hurry or feel there will be plenty of time to say the words later."

She glanced back at him, questions forming on her beautiful features. "You're being cryptic."

"Dinner is getting cold."

She didn't move, blink, or act like she heard him, and he immediately wondered what she was thinking. He didn't have to wait long. "Why do you cringe every time Asher calls me Madilyn?"

When he didn't answer, she inhaled a heavy breath. "You're right. Dinner is getting cold."

****

Asher insisted on carrying their dinner plates to the kitchen and set them in the sink. "Dinner was delicious, Madilyn." He took off his jacket and started rolling up his sleeves.

She jumped into action as Brice brought a couple of glasses into the kitchen. "Don't worry about those. Let's all go into the living room, and I'll make us some coffee."

Brice set the glasses by the sink. "That would be good."

"I stopped drinking coffee a few years ago, but I'd enjoy staying a while." Asher took his jacket from the counter and laid it on the back of the couch.

Small cries filtered into the kitchen, and Brice touched her hip in passing. "I'll check on her. Be back in a minute."

She nodded. "Thank you."

Asher smiled at her as she entered the living room. "I'm glad you're here for the wedding. Amabelle mentioned you were to be a bridesmaid but wasn't sure if you'd make it. It would've been a pleasure to walk you down the aisle."

The implication formed a knot in her throat. "Yes, well, with my job…"

His brows knitted together. "Still working at the police station?"

Asher had no clue about her real work. Several years ago, he'd overheard a conversation she was having with Amabelle and Patrick and assumed she worked at the police station. They were the only ones who knew the truth, and they never corrected him, but once again hearing the disapproval in Asher's voice hurt. "I am."

"Have you ever thought about doing something else?"

"No. Not really. My work is fulfilling, and I enjoy what I do."

"I can't help but be concerned for your wellbeing, and now that I'm partner, I can provide the type of life we've talked about."

Stunned, Madi rose slowly from the couch and glanced toward her bedroom where Brice had gone. Memories of Asher's broken promises filled her.

Asher stood. "Madilyn, I know things didn't work out before—"

"Wait." She held out her hand. "Please don't say another word. I'm not sure where this is coming from, but there's been some kind of misunderstanding." She had to think. Did she say something to cause this? Inviting him to dinner? Wasn't having Brice in her bedroom a signal or red flag where she was concerned?

"There's no mistake. I told you after I made partner we'd marry. I haven't forgotten."

"Asher, that was after high school graduation. You went your way and I went mine." It's what she'd told herself after she found out he was seeing someone else.

"That was a long time ago. We can't just pick up where we left off."

"Does this have to do with Brice?"

Yes. No. "It has to do with you leaving for Boston. You quit returning my calls. Quit coming home like you said, and there were too many broken promises. You moved on, remember?"

He looked to the floor, then to her. "Things were so different in Boston. The atmosphere. The people… If I could turn back time, I'd do things differently. I'd do things the right way—with you."

"It's been ten or eleven years since we were together."

"I know it's a lot to ask, especially with another man in your bedroom, but I've thought about this for a while. Haven't you noticed every time you make it home, I'm not far behind? Can't we start over? When I look at my sister and see what she and Patrick have gone through to get where they are today, I believe they'd say it was worth it. They found each other again, and they are more in love now than ever."

Asher took a step closer and ran a hand down her arm. "I want another chance, Madilyn."

She moved from his touch, and his hand fell.

"Will you at least think about it? Please. Give us some thought before you answer. If for nothing else, out of respect for our friendship. I know it means something to you regardless of time."

Their history was long with memories so wrapped up in each other that at one time she didn't know where one began and the other ended. But she didn't love him any longer, not like that.

Friends. Family. Yes.

She opened her mouth to explain, but Asher pulled her into a hug and her body went stiff.

"It's late," he said, letting her go. He grabbed his jacket from the couch, crushing the collar as he started for the door. "I'll give you time to think."

Madi followed him to the foyer, dumbfounded, needing to stop him before he got his hopes up. "Asher."

He glanced toward her bedroom and cleared his throat. "Where is Brice staying?"

"Um, here, but it's not what you might be thinking." She shut her mouth before she said too much.

"I'll call you." He pulled the door open, and the cold air brought a chill to her bones. "Bye, Madilyn. See you soon." He closed the door, and she quickly moved into the living room.

Madi closed her eyes, annoyed at having been so easily derailed.

Brice came to mind. How would she explain this to him? Grabbing the throw from the rocker, she tossed it across her shoulders and headed into her bedroom.

With Abby being a light sleeper, she took extra care entering her room. She squinted against the bathroom light she'd left on, catching sight of Brice in her recliner with Abby sprawled over his chest, asleep.

What a picture they made. Abby's tiny hand palmed his bicep, covering portions of his tattoo. Her brown wavy hair was now matted against his chest, and a smile lifted Madi's lips.

They looked so peaceful that Madi hated to move her, but she slipped the baby from Brice's arms and laid her in the play yard.

"Hey," he whispered. "She had a hard time going back to sleep."

"Thank you for taking care of her."

"Asher?"

"He left." She covered Abby with her blanket, then

straightened, watching her small chest rise and fall.

She sensed Brice's presence behind her though he never said a word. She took strength from him as she always had, but tonight it felt wrong, like she was stealing. "Thank you again. I hope you sleep well."

"I'm not going to bed when something is bothering you."

"Stunned and confused is more like it. I thought coming here for my brother's wedding would be nice, normal. Nothing about this trip has been normal."

Brice placed a hand on her waist and led her out of the bedroom, releasing her once they were in the hallway. "Want some coffee?"

Madi nodded and followed him into the kitchen, where the dirty dishes remained. She yanked the dishwasher open and began adding silverware.

"Want to talk about it?"

When she didn't answer, she felt his gaze like a beam, aimed right for her heart.

She continued with the dishes.

After a few minutes, Brice held up their cups.

"Coffee's ready. Come sit."

"I won't be good company."

"It never bothered me before." He grinned, yet his eyes held concern as he gave a nod toward the living room.

She was almost finished with the dishes but washed her hands instead and joined him on the couch. After taking the coffee mug from him, she began rearranging the pillows at her back and added distance between them.

He said nothing as he watched her, but the intensity in his gaze grew. "Talk to me, Madi."

"I don't know where to begin."

"The beginning will do."

She took a deep breath and looked down at her coffee. "Asher and I dated in high school."

"I had a feeling you might have dated."

"We weren't the popular kids. People weren't rushing to break down our doors and ask us to prom. So for my sophomore and Asher's junior year, we decided to go to prom together. Shortly after prom, we started dating. It was odd at first because we'd been friends since kindergarten. The next year came along, and we began discussing our hopes and dreams for our future."

"Marriage and family?"

Madi nodded. "With his senior prom and graduation in the books, we started making plans, where we'd live, how many children we wanted. But after he left for Boston, things started to change. He came home less. His calls were fewer. We struggled to make a long-distance relationship work, and I couldn't figure out why. But I was young, in love, and I believed in forever." She took a sip of her coffee and gave herself a moment before plunging forward through the memories and hurt they had caused each other.

"I started noticing a pattern—when he called, when I couldn't reach him—so I traveled to Boston. When I arrived at his apartment, his roommate said he was gone for the weekend with his girlfriend."

"I'm sorry."

"It hurt more than I thought possible." She paused, taking another sip. "He came home once he found out I knew, but I was already gone. I had a friend who moved to D.C. and was looking for a roommate. I packed up my things and headed out."

"Did he look for you? Didn't your family tell him where you went?"

"They keep my secret. It's the reason Patrick and

Amabelle know I work as an undercover agent. They still don't know more than that, but I trusted them then as I do now. However, he did come looking for me over the years."

She smiled thinking back. "Once, about five years ago, the agency put a tail on him because they thought he might have been a threat." She met Brice's gaze. "Asher thinks I work for my local police department. He hates the idea. Says I shouldn't put myself in harm's way. I can't imagine what he'd think if he knew the truth."

"How often have you seen him since?"

"I saw him for the first time about four years ago. I came home, and he was visiting Amabelle. I see him about once a year. Our conversations are pretty normal. Weather, family, job, those types of things."

"Not tonight it seems."

"No. Not tonight."

"What did he say to upset you?"

"I'm not upset."

"You're twisting your ring."

She placed her hands in her lap and tried not to fidget. It was next to impossible. "He said he still loves me..."

The emotionless look in Brice's eyes and face gave away none of his feelings. She probably had no right, but she wanted some type of reaction. Did Brice even care? Did her words affect him at all?

She blew out a frustrated breath and continued. "He told me he wanted a second chance, asked me to think about it before I make my decision. Then he went on to remind me about Patrick and Amabelle and all they'd gone through."

"And now they're marrying." Brice drank the last of his coffee. "He's looking at others to see what's best for you?"

Madi had to admit she'd done the same. She shrugged. "I guess."

"What about the other night? Us?"

"Everything I said was and is still true. Nothing has changed."

"But Asher wants you back, and you agreed to think about it." Brice rose slowly from the couch.

"Wait a minute." She stood. "Sort of. I tried to discourage him."

He turned to leave but paused. "I know I'm not forthcoming with my feelings, and I should have shared more of them before now, but this thing between us, I want to see where it takes us. I'm thankful for the first day you walked into my life, Madi. And every day since. I'm not ready for you to walk out of it."

He went into the kitchen, set his cup in the sink, and disappeared around the corner. A second later, a door clicked in the distance.

CHAPTER EIGHT

After flicking on the bathroom light, Brice squinted, catching a glimpse of a yellow sticky note attached to the mirror. He blinked to clear the sleep from his eyes and leaned in.

My given name is Madilyn. Why does it bother you when Asher uses it?

He took a heavy breath and ran his fingers through his hair. He'd gone to bed thinking of Asher and Madi. He didn't want to think about Asher first thing.

Besides, he was out of his league here, a note stuck to the mirror asking him what he felt. He felt plenty. But how would he explain it without coming off too direct? Give him a gun and point to the enemy, and he could handle it. That was instinctive. He commanded, willingly to die for the Lord, his country, and his brothers at his side. How did a man fight with a pen and sticky note?

He brushed his teeth, trying to figure out what to write. He decided right then and there to say what he felt, and if anyone was to be at her side, he'd hope he was the one. The only one to call her *Madilyn*.

He went into his room, snagged a pen from the desk, and returned to the bathroom. On the sticky note he scribbled, *It's your given name, Madi. It's personal, intimate. If I have the honor one day, it will be used on our wedding night.*

It was time to fight for what he wanted.

The doorbell rang, jerking him to attention. He glanced across the hall to where the gun rested on the nightstand, then hurried to the front door and caught sight of Amabelle through the window. He inspected his black pajama pants and white tee, making sure he was presentable enough.

He swung the door open. "Good morning," he greeted, inhaling a cleansing breath of cool air.

Amabelle rubbed her hands together. A gust of wind blew against her back, sending her brown hair whipping in her face. "It's gotten colder."

"Please, come in."

She tightened her jacket, stepping into the foyer, and he closed the door behind her. "Is Madi still asleep?"

"I'm not sure. I've not seen her this morning. She was up late last night."

Amabelle tucked several flyaway strands of hair behind her ear. "I heard my brother stopped by."

"He did. I was about to make coffee. Would you care for a cup? Breakfast?"

"I'm fine, thank you. It seems a storm is coming in, and I wanted to get Abby. After yesterday, I'd hate to get caught on the road. Patrick reminded me it was still a drive out here. And speaking of Patrick, he's invited Asher, you, and Madi over for lunch tomorrow about noon." She hooked a thumb over her shoulder. "Mind if I use the bathroom before I get Abby?"

"Please, feel free. And Abby's in Madi's room." Brice walked into the kitchen but then stopped, dread filling

53

him.

The sticky note.

He rubbed the back of his neck and glanced toward the bathroom. There was nothing he could do about it now or the fact that Asher's sister was probably reading it.

He grabbed himself a glass and was filling it with water when Amabelle emerged, holding back a smile. "I wasn't expecting company," he said.

"I noticed. Love your answer, by the way."

"Thanks. No hard feelings with Asher being your brother?"

"None when I know they aren't right for each other. Madi knows they aren't, but my brother has a way of convincing people to his way of thinking. He's a great lawyer. Besides, notes like that will remind Madi of the truth."

"I hope you're right."

"Trust me." She smiled and left for Abby, giving him time to think.

How should he give Madi his answer? Hand it to her and wait until she read it? Nah, too awkward.

Place it on her mirror as she had his? But how would he get it there when they didn't share a bathroom?

Amabelle returned with a sleepy Abby on one shoulder, diaper bag on the other, dragging the play yard in its carrying case.

He went to her, taking the play yard and bag. "Let me help you. There's also the other car seat in my car." He held the door and assisted them to the car. After he placed Amabelle's things in the trunk and backseat, he stopped next to her open window.

"About my brother, I don't want you to think I don't love him," she said. "I do dearly, and I want what's best for him, but Madi needs someone who's attentive, compassionate. She deserves someone who will love her beyond hope, beyond circumstances. A sacrificial type of love. Like Christ... My brother can't offer her that. Perhaps you can. I'll be praying for you both."

"Thank you."

"Hopefully we'll see you tomorrow." The window rolled up, and she backed out of the driveway.

Taken by Amabelle's honesty, Brice stepped into the house just as Madi barreled toward the door. Stunned, he caught her against him.

"Abby's gone!" She searched his eyes and gripped his shirt.

"She's safe. Amabelle was here. A few minutes ago. They're on their way home now." The pulse in her neck raced and her eyes glazed over. A moment later, her grip lightened and she palmed his chest with both hands.

He was tempted to tug her closer but resisted as she took a step back. "She said there's a storm approaching and wanted to come early."

"Makes sense." She fingered her hair, which seemed to be part of her morning routine when she hadn't had a chance to run a brush through the waves.

His routine was breathing. However, today he wanted the privilege of his hands running through her hair and untangling the knots. To tell her things he'd bottled up inside and explore how kissing her would taste.

"Um, let me shower, and I'll work on breakfast." She started for her room.

"Madi, wait." Brice went into the bathroom and came back out with the sticky note, bending it so she'd understand not to read it until she entered her bedroom. He'd never considered himself a coward until this moment.

He held it out to her. "Your answer."

Madi regarded the paper. "Are you sure you want me to read it?"

Okay, so maybe she shouldn't. *Yes, she should.* What was wrong with him? This woman was turning him inside out. "Do you really want to know?"

"I do." She took the note, grazing his thumb in the process. "I wasn't sure you were going to respond."

"After our conversation last night, I thought I should."

She dipped her head slightly, glancing at the note between her slim fingers. "Thank you."

She headed in the direction of her room. Her long, knotted hair tumbled over her shoulders and the extra-large T-shirt that sagged off her shoulders revealed the slope of her neck and soft skin. The thought of his answer seemed very attainable until her door closed in the distance, waking him from his daydream.

What had he been thinking?

CHAPTER NINE

Breakfast had been over two hours ago and here Madi sat in her recliner, staring at her phone in one hand and a sticky note in the other. Yesterday, Asher wanted her to think about marriage. Today, he'd texted twice asking if he could see her or meet up for lunch. And then Adam, her supervisor, asked her to pack up and head to Vienna early. She wasn't going. Her brother's wedding was too important.

Men.

Madi reread Brice's words for the fifth time, memorizing the flow of his script, absorbing the words to heart.

Another text from Asher came through.

I'm not trying to push you, Madilyn. I only miss you. We need to meet for lunch.

This wasn't going to work. She couldn't go to lunch with him. Brice would sit with them or at a table close by. This was a conversation she needed to have alone. She had to tell Asher she wasn't interested, but not today.

She texted back. *Patrick said for us to come over tomorrow. We can get together then.*

I want time alone with you. I want us to talk.

Her sentiments exactly. *Then we can go for a walk.*

There was a pause, and Madi was about to set her phone down when another text came through.

Is that my only option?

Yes.

Then let's go for a walk. I know the perfect spot. Hey, I gotta go. Talk to you tonight.

Madi dropped her phone in her lap. She reached up to rub her forehead, and the sticky note scratched the top of her nose. With a sigh, she ripped it off her hand, stuck it to the bottom of her button-down shirt, and stood. It was time to talk with Brice.

Seeing the pile of colored sticky notes on her desk gave her an idea to keep Brice talking. She grabbed a stack and an extra pen.

She found Brice sitting on the back deck, looking out over the property. She set the notes and extra pen on the coffee table and pulled the door open. "Wow, it's gotten cold." She stepped into the frigid air.

Brice stood and took off what looked like a ski jacket and wrapped it around her shoulders. The size of it swallowed her whole. "Do you want to go in?"

At first, she thought she did, but now with Brice's jacket keeping her warm, she wanted to stay. "Fresh air will do me good." She pulled one of her patio chairs out from the table and sat with him. "Would you like your jacket back? I can grab a quilt."

"Keep it. I'm fine. It's like summer, remember?"

"You wear a ski jacket during summer?" She tilted her head, catching his smile, and what a handsome smile it was. "I love it here. The wide-open spaces. Deer roam free. Oh, you should see spring. It's my favorite time of year. Everything begins to bloom. The flowers, the trees. It's breathtaking."

"If that's an invitation, I might take you up on your offer."

"Hopefully, next time you'll come of your own accord and not to be my bodyguard." She glanced down, seeing his note attached to her shirt. What a change of events in the last few days. She peeled it off and held it out for him. "This wasn't what I had expected."

He slipped his hand overs hers and ran his thumb over her knuckles. "What were you expecting?"

"Nothing like this." She couldn't believe this was happening, but as she watched his thumb caress her fingers, the sun spot on her hand, and return to her knuckles, the truth froze her in place. This was indeed happening.

"Are you disappointed?"

"No, just surprised." She slid her palm from his, kicking herself for letting go, and shoved her hands into his jacket pockets. "I've known for a long time you've cared about me."

"Deeply."

"But marriage?"

"Bodyguard to marriage is a long jump." He shifted in his chair and exhaled. The plume of warm air from his mouth became visible. "It doesn't mean my feelings weren't there."

"You've hidden them well."

"I've had to learn. On the battlefield, feelings and emotions can cause mistakes. Most of the time I hold them back and try not to express them, to keep control. Just because a soldier is back on American soil doesn't change the way he learned to survive."

His last sentence sounded like... She studied him, his eyes. "I can read you at times. You're very focused, driven. Intense. Like a moment ago, but now you seem relaxed. Content."

"Don't let me fool you. Yes, I'm content right now. You're safe. I enjoy being with you, but relaxed? Not so much." He looked out to the yard. "Opening up isn't easy."

She tightened the jacket around her. "I'll let you in on a little secret of my own. I've been clinging to hope that one day there might be an us. It's grown harder though in the past months. You were pushing me away, and I was starting to think—"

Brice stood and collected her hand, helping her to stand. "You're freezing. Let's go inside." He placed a palm on her back and held the door open for her. "Why don't we have a fire in the fireplace? It's cold enough."

"That would be nice. I miss having a fire. My little apartment in North Carolina leaves a lot to be desired." She slipped off his jacket, missing the warmth it provided along with its clean outdoorsy scent.

"Then we'll solve that problem. I saw a pile of cut firewood outside. I'll be right back."

She handed him his jacket. "You'll need this."

"Save it for me." He shot her a rare smile and darted out the door.

She went weak in the knees and leaned against the door frame, pressing his jacket collar to her nose. *He's thought about being married to me? What other things has he thought of?* She glanced to the sticky notes and extra pen she'd placed on the coffee table.

Seeing Brice coming her way carrying a massive load of wood in his arms, she threw the jacket to the couch and opened the door for him. She shivered as the wind rushed into the room, then kicked the door closed behind him.

The muscles in Brice's arms tightened under the

weight. She allowed herself the pleasure of watching him build a fire, listening to the crack and pop of the wood.

As the light of the flame glowed, licking the wood and pine cones, he smiled over his shoulder. "Almost there. You'll be warm soon."

She was reminded once again of how stunning he was. Handsome. Powerful in physical strength, but also how he drew respect from all who knew him, straight up the military and government ladder. His dedication and commitment were like none she'd ever witnessed before. She was surprised the two words weren't tattooed on his chest because he acted as if they were medals on a uniform.

And love—she hadn't expected it. She'd hoped for it no matter how much he pushed her away. Yet, here was Brice on hand and knee making a fire because he desired to make her happy. She tilted her head and watched as he rose and stoked the flames, her mind enlightening with the truth. Why hadn't she noticed before? His love language was service.

She pressed her hand to her cheek in amazement. Brice had been doing random things… Such as a year ago when she'd added new flooring in her apartment, he wanted to help. Or when she'd needed a lift to work because her car broke down.

Her mind filled with Brice's other acts of service. He'd surprised her by having the car taken to the shop and fixed. She'd paid him of course, but he fought her before finally giving in. There were little things too, the way he made sure she ate during their stakeouts by bringing her favorites to snack on…

All this time, he had loved her.

As if a floodgate opened, she wanted to jump for joy, share the news with anyone who'd listen, and throw her arms around Brice and tell him exactly how she felt in return.

Now isn't the best time for that type of reaction. Get a grip, Madi. Take this slow.

Brice planted a hand on the mantle, looking down at the flames, then at her. "You'll warm faster over here."

She stood alongside him and held out her hands. The chill that still clung to her vanished. "Feels divine."

"Did you cut yourself?" He pivoted to her and cupped her face, tilting it down slightly. He ran a finger along the bridge of her nose.

Stunned, she blinked up at him, trying to recall the question. "Oh, yes, but it's nothing. It was your sticky note."

"Bringing it closer to read in case you misread it the first time?"

"I admit, I read it a few times." She smiled, and his gaze fell to her mouth. Whether it was the heat from the fire or the way Brice was looking at her, she moved from the fireplace before she caught on fire. She strolled to the coffee table and collected the sticky notes and pens before lowering to the foot of the couch.

"What do you have there? More questions?" He sat beside her but on the couch.

She began separating the sticky notes by color. "Yes, I thought since last time worked so well, why not." She held up a rainbow of choices. "Pick your color."

He picked blue.

Madi should have known he would since it was his favorite color. She kept the stack of sea greens. Handing him a pen over her shoulder, she leaned back against his legs. "How about we start with two. Whatever we ask each other, we're required to answer. Sound fair?"

"Are you sure you want to do this?" His blue eyes

sparkled in the fire's light, and she wasn't sure of anything at the moment.

She turned away, thinking of a question that didn't include why had he waited so long to tell her that he was in love with her. "Are you scared?"

He was scribbling something behind her. "No."

Silence and the crackling of the fire filled the living room as did the scent of cedar. Taken by the moment and the surreal fact Brice was next to her, she almost sighed with pleasure, but then a question came to mind, then another. She began writing.

"Finished?" he asked when she set the pen on the floor beside her.

"I think so." She leaned back and glanced up. Brice was leaning over her, smiling.

He ran a finger across her hairline. "You first."

This was a bad idea.

CHAPTER TEN

Even upside-down, Brice could see the indecision playing across Madi's features. "You've decided not to go through with it?"

She wouldn't look at him. "Maybe it's better if we don't, or at least let me change my question."

What type of questions could she possibly ask that were harder than the one he'd been given earlier? "I'm sure I can handle whatever you want to ask." But at her hesitation, he began to wonder.

"Are you sure?"

"Of course."

Madi handed him her green sticky note.

Do you have PTSD?

His mouth went dry, and he frowned at the question, wanting to throw it in the fire, along with his flashbacks, sleepless nights, and the war he battled within. He wanted it to burn, smolder, before he collected its ashes and threw them into the sea. The Lord would do it one day, throw the hell of this earth into the abyss. He couldn't wait for that day.

"After each of my tours, I've had to go through several extensive evaluations. I have never been diagnosed with PTSD."

Madi was tossing his answer around in her mind. The

way she twisted her ring was proof enough. She only did that when she was upset or in deep thought, and he assumed the latter.

He rose to his feet, unable to stay seated, and knew the moment he did he was giving himself away. Madi was a smart woman. They worked well together because they knew each other, how to read one another. Sometimes they were able to hide things from each other, like his love for her, but it was a constant battle he no longer had to fight. What would it be like to not have to hide anything from one person in this world? The Lord knew. What would that mean if he told her and she walked away?

The answer would be clear. She truly wasn't the one. But what would happen if she stayed and he became worse? How would she handle it when he could barely deal with it now?

She came up behind him and stood there for a moment. Madi at this point would assess the damage and find a way to control it. As a fixer, it was what she did. But she wouldn't be able to fix him.

Her hand settled along his waist, and he flinched against her touch. "I'm here. You can tell me anything."

"This is why I kept you away. If you knew the truth... I could lose you, Madi. So I put just enough distance between us to still hold on to you."

Madi rested her head on his back, and her other hand came around his waist. "I'm not going anywhere," she whispered.

His eyes closed at the need to save Madi from herself. His desire for her was stronger, yet he fought it. "It's getting worse. The flashbacks. The nights are getting longer."

She released him and pulled him around to face her. "I

know what I'm doing."

"You don't have a clue."

"I might not, but I know you have episodes. I've been through one with you, and if you let me, I'll be there for you through more."

He cupped her cheek, his thumb running a line along her jaw. "You're driving me insane."

"You can kiss me when we're done talking."

He smiled at that and ran his thumb over her bottom lip. "Promise me?"

"Promise me you'll get help."

He dropped his hand and stepped back. "I don't know if I can."

"Why can't you? There are treatments out there that have helped others."

"It's not that."

"Then tell me."

"I could lose my job. No more Homeland Security. Then how can I protect you? Do you understand how that would affect me, not being there, not knowing if you're safe?"

"What else?"

"Once I step foot in an office and admit to having PTSD, I will always be labeled. I'd still be the same man, but people will look at me differently. It's not that I don't want the help, I do. I just don't want my life to change because of PTSD. I left half of myself on the battlefield. I don't want the rest of me to be taken away too."

Madi walked to the couch and lifted both of his sticky notes. She read them slowly as she reached him and held out the first one. "*What will I tell Asher?* Honestly, I've thought about it since he called this morning."

"He called this morning? I thought he was giving you time?"

"I guess his timing and mine are different." She wadded up the note and tossed it in the fire. "We're having lunch with Patrick and Amabelle tomorrow. Asher will be there so I told him we can go for a walk and talk about things."

"Where do you plan on walking?" He went to the fireplace and added more wood, stoking the fire.

"I'm not sure, but he had a place in mind. I think he'll probably take me to a large boulder near the creek. It's on Patrick's property. I'll be safe so you won't have to worry."

Brice pulled at the fabric of her shirt, drawing her into his arms. "I can't help but worry. Two years I've been your bodyguard. It's hard to shut down the need to protect you when we're not undercover." He tucked her hair behind her ear, mesmerized by her beauty. "Have you really not dated anyone since Asher? I know you've been asked."

Madi held up his blue sticky note. "I don't believe that question is on this paper." She stuck it to his chest and read the note. *Do you know how to dance?* I actually have the same question on one of mine."

"How about we dance and find out?"

She smiled at him. "There's no music."

Brice laced his fingers through hers, not wanting to part from her, and walked them to where his phone rested on the kitchen counter. He found a station and set it for continual play. "We do now."

****

Madi led Brice back into the living room, and as she turned and faced him, fought a laugh at his slightly dipped brows. "What are you thinking about?"

He slid his hand along her waist, his other along the length of her hair. "You. I don't understand it. Why haven't you dated? Because of Asher?"

"Yes and no. When Asher and I broke it off, it devastated me. But I learned a valuable lesson."

"What lesson?"

"That I didn't want to date, but if I did, God had to pick the man for me. I'm not standing here with you wanting a boyfriend. I'm standing here wondering if you're the man I'm going to marry. I guess you can say this is my response to your first sticky note."

"I'm not sure if I should run or take the kiss I've been after all night."

She gave him a smirk. "I think we should dance. You ready? I'll let you lead."

Brice chuckled. "I appreciate it."

After a few steps, Madi was grinning at him. She couldn't help herself. Brice always seemed to amaze her. "You can dance."

"You're forced to learn when you've been a groomsman at countless weddings." He spun her and with perfect timing, drew her close, sliding his hand along her back. Step by step, he led and she followed.

His eyes smiled. "Ready."

"Absolutely."

He turned her out and spun her twice, then brought her back into his arms. "You're a great dancer yourself."

"I guess we're in the same shoes. I'm always the bridesmaid, never the bride."

"You know what that means, right? We're going to rock at the chicken dance."

The way his blue eyes crinkled at the edges, taking her in, she didn't want this day to end. "We will, won't we?"

"The best." He winked and leaned her back into a dip.

"Now to sweep you off your feet."

****

The glow from the fireplace had dimmed and the cold was beginning to envelop Brice as he stabbed the poker at the dying flames. They reminded him of a different night, one when his team crowded into a huddle.

He closed his eyes against the memories skimming his consciousness. Instead, he focused on the way Madi was tonight. The way she laughed. Danced. Loved him.

He loved her with everything that was within him. If he was diagnosed with PTSD, he'd be pulled from the case. Then who would protect her? Her life was more important than his need for her.

Madi's bedroom door creaked. He bowed his head to glance at the timber still smoldering in the fireplace.

"Hey. You're still awake."

He looked up at her and gave a half-smile. "Have some things on my mind. And you?"

She tightened her robe and tucked back her hair from her face. "Same." She pointed at the floor in front of him. "Do you mind if I sit?"

He lifted his hand for hers, regretting it as her palm molded within his. With her back to him, she leaned into his chest. He closed his eyes, feeling the nearness, the warmth of her body.

"I had a wonderful time tonight."

"Me too."

She chuckled. "I think Mr. and Mrs. Shafer will be very convincing."

"I'm sure they will. Minus the kissing."

She turned her body slightly and gazed up at him. "Then I think we should practice."

His gaze fell to her lips. Before his brain caught up with his body, his mouth found hers. His fingers wove through her hair and roamed to the back of her neck. He brought her closer, deepening their kiss. His brain finally caught up and he began to pull away, but her mouth found his again.

She whispered, "I love you."

Her words, the feel of her, set up a constant give and take of kisses, touches, and their desperate need for air.

"Madi," he breathed, finally taking control. He rested his head against hers, fighting for his feelings to submit and follow in step with what needed to be done.

"I love you," she repeated. "I don't know how it happened. I never saw you coming. But I do." She ran her hand along his arm, kissing his chin, the corner of his mouth.

"Madi," he moaned. "I need coffee."

She giggled next his ear. "Coffee?"

His eyes closed against the feel of her. "Or if you want to make homemade biscuits, cook a five-course meal, I'm in."

She pulled back and smiled at him. "You know I don't cook."

"You want to give it a shot tonight?"

"No," she chuckled, and as she started to stand, he offered his hand to help. "But coffee should give us enough time to collect ourselves."

He tugged at her hand, drawing her a step. He kissed her knuckles. "Thank you."

"You always put me first, don't you?"

"I try, but sometimes it's hard." She squeezed his fingers, and Brice waited for Madi to enter the kitchen before he stood. He strolled over to the fireplace and stoked the fire, adding wood. He blew on the dying embers and the flames licked the bottom of the newly placed kindling. He blew again, the heat building, reminding him of what he and Madi shared a moment ago.

Better a heated room than their kisses, he decided now that he could think clearly. He loved her, and loving someone called for respect. And if he had to protect her from himself, he would.

A few minutes later, Madi came from the kitchen with two mugs in her hands. "You got the fire going again."

"You don't mind, do you?"

"Of course not."

He took both mugs from her. "Why don't we sit on the couch."

"Sure."

He lowered next to her and handed over her mug.

Madi sat against him. "I think I could stare at the fire all night." She took a sip.

"Would you like to? I can hold you until morning."

She leaned her head back slightly, and her lips parted.

It took him a nanosecond to realize what his words might have meant coming from another man. "Nothing more," he said.

"I'm not worried." She kissed the edge of his jaw, then took another sip of her coffee. "Can I ask you something?"

"Sure."

"What were you thinking about when I first came in?"

His body went stiff. Madi was perceptive. Had he revealed too much of himself and what he was feeling? Surely she sensed his discomfort at her question. If she hadn't known something was off before, she did now. "Why?"

She shrugged. "I've seen that phantom gaze of yours

before, the night I watched the sunrise with you." She inhaled a long breath. "Let me in."

What could he say? Not the truth, not all of it anyway. He didn't know how to say the words. How did he explain there was a tight rope the same length as the ocean he was stumbling across that held his past and the future? There had never been a net beneath him. Madi wanted to be that net.

Yes, she'd try to save him, but would he pull her with him like a drowning man vying for a final breath, plummeting both to their deaths? "I want you here with me ... I need you here with me."

"I'm not going anywhere."

****

"Sir! Over there!" Goolsby caught his attention.

Shots fired over his head and zipped past his ear. Brice's focus landed where Goolsby pointed. Taliban were heading toward them—

A hand gripped his shoulder. Brice bolted awake, throwing the enemy off him. He jumped to his feet, ready to fight.

His chest filled with air. The sight of Madi on the floor, gaping in shock. Glass lay shattered around her from the water glass on the coffee table. Blood coming from her fingers.

He fell hard on his knees at her side. His mind swirled. "Oh, Madi. I'm sorry. So sorry." How could he help? Make this right? "Let me see."

Her movement was slow as she sat up, but the blood was sure. He ripped off his shirt and held it against the wound.

She flinched and a moan escaped.

How could he right this? He couldn't. He was the reason she was injured.

Madi hunched over her knees. "I'm fine. Stunned is all, really. I hit my head on the table."

"I'm going to look." He moved his shirt, and with the edge, wiped the blood from the area. "You're going to need some pain meds." Next, he examined the back of her head and the bump forming there.

"I think you're right. How's it look?"

"Like someone threw you against a table and you hit your head."

"It feels like it too." She chuckled, then winced.

Brice didn't see the humor in it. She was making jokes when it could have been worse. The thought of what he was capable of—even to the woman he loved—made him cringe. He scooped her legs up with one hand and held her close with the other.

"What are you doing?"

"Taking you to the couch."

"I'm not helpless."

"You're not, but this is my fault." He set her down and tried to make her as comfortable as possible. "I'll get those pain meds."

He wasn't in the kitchen more than a minute when Madi came in and headed straight for a cabinet. She reached in, grabbed a medicine bottle, and a small smirk lifted her mouth. Popping two pills in her mouth, she downed a cup of water he gave her.

"I think I'll get a bag of ice for my head. Why don't you put another shirt on and meet me on the couch."

He took the cup from her and set it in the sink. "I think I'm heading to bed after I clean up the glass. You should do the same. I'm going to check on you every two hours to make sure you're all right."

"I don't care about the mess. And I'm fine. I have a headache. So what. The swelling will go down. I've had worse."

"Not because of me. Do you have any idea...?" He took a step back and ran his fingers through his hair.

"Brice."

He couldn't do this. If he ever hurt her again... But there was someone who wouldn't. Someone who wanted to give her a life that he couldn't. She'd loved the man once. Maybe if she gave him another chance... "When you see Asher tomorrow...tell him you need more time."

Her body flinched. "What?"

"This thing between us, it's a mistake."

"So, your kissing me, holding me was a mistake?" Hurt and anger filled her eyes, and he hated himself for it.

"This won't work between us."

"I'm not sure at what point you checked out of this evening or the last two years, but we work great together. And this thing between us, it's called love. In my book, it's worth fighting for."

This wasn't going well. He wanted her to yell or walk away. But the more she fought him and the more determined that mind of hers became, the more he needed her. "I'll ruin us. Don't you understand?"

"You're trying to ruin us now."

He shoved his hands into his pockets. "No, I'm saving you from heartache. From pain. From what's it's like having to live with someone like me."

"Someone like you?" She walked to him and placed a hand along his face. "You're loyal, devoted, my protector, but you're also a fighter. You talk about people labeling you because of PTSD. It sounds as if you've already done it. You have a choice how you want to live that future."

"Madi." He collected her palm from his face, unable to

handle the feel of her gentleness toward him. "You deserve someone better." He let her go, and her hand fell to her side.

"I guess I'm surprised is all. A man like you who's fought for your country in ways I can't begin to comprehend, yet you're not willing to fight a little longer. For freedom. For yourself. For us."

"I'm tired of fighting."

"Then you're in the wrong occupation. And maybe you're right, I deserve someone better."

Brice steeled himself at her words. Only a few days ago, he told her he wasn't ready for her to walk out of his life. He wanted to see where this thing between them would go. And now here he was watching Madi leave the room. She never glanced back, and he deserved it. A man that hurt a woman didn't deserve to breathe.

CHAPTER ELEVEN

Madi fumed as she finished dressing for lunch with her family. She still couldn't believe Brice would encourage her toward Asher. What was he thinking? He wasn't, she decided.

Her loyal, devoted protector was frightened. Why didn't she think of it before? Everyone becomes frightened of something at some point in their lives. That something for Brice obviously wasn't the thought of losing her.

She stood in front of the full-length mirror and turned her backside to the glass. She hadn't worn these gray jeans in over a year. Thankfully, they still fit because she loved the way they'd look with her white sweater and brown boots. And so would Brice.

In all her thirty-four years, not once had she tried to attract a man, except for while working, but that didn't count. This counted. Brice counted.

"Lord, I don't know what today will hold, but I know you hold my future. Show me how to help Brice. Reveal in me your peace regardless of what might happen or be said. Thank you, Lord. Thank you for being faithful."

She glanced at herself once again as she passed by the mirror. Her pulse rose in anticipation of the day, and she fingered her ring. Catching herself, she looked to her hand, slid the silver ring off, and set it on her dresser. The less Brice knew how she was feeling, the better.

****

"Brice, welcome to our home." Patrick shook his hand and led him and Madi into the living room where Asher stood.

"Thank you for the invitation." He glanced around the spacious home, forcing himself not to focus on Asher taking Madi's hands within his and commenting on how beautiful she looked.

Amabelle came from the bedroom carrying Abby, but once Abby saw Madi, the little girl stretched out for her.

"Come here, sweetie." Madi kissed her cheek and fingered a few strands of her hair. "Did Mommy just change your diaper?"

"I did." Amabelle gave Madi a side hug and turned her gaze to Brice, smiling. "I hope y'all are hungry. I made a feast for the first time in our kitchen."

Patrick opened the oven and withdrew a pan of cordon bleu. "She cooked my favorite. Hope you don't mind."

"Not at all." Asher placed a palm on Madi's back and led her to the dining room, where he pulled out her chair and sat beside her.

Brice stiffened as he joined everyone. He got stuck sitting next to Asher. Patrick sat on his other side, but Brice didn't mind. He liked the man and felt some sort of camaraderie even though they'd only met. However, things would be different if Patrick ever found out what happened between him and Madi last night.

"Amabelle, I love how you decorated the table for Christmas. Your table runner is beautiful." Madi fingered the fabric with a sweet childlike wistfulness to her expression.

"Our mom made it years ago," Asher said and lifted his glass of water.

Abby batted her plastic spoon on her highchair tray, and Patrick chuckled. "I think someone wants to say the prayer and eat."

Everyone held hands without being prompted, and Brice looked to Madi, wondering why she hadn't mentioned this part. Maybe it had something to do with her barely saying two words to him since she'd walked away last night. But when had he given her a chance?

Madi must have sensed his awkwardness because she gave him a smile. Yet, regardless of how perfectly she smiled or how it affected him, he still didn't want to hold Asher's hand. Biting the bullet, he listened as Patrick prayed. His prayer for Brice and Madi took him by surprise. For a moment, he considered what it might be like to be part of their family, but as his eyes opened, Asher's hand moved to Madi's, and that picture shattered into hundreds of pieces.

All during lunch, Amabelle and Madi talked about the wedding while Patrick and Asher discussed the honeymoon. Brice took everything in—the excitement in Patrick's tone, Amabelle's bright eyes as she described the bridal gown Madi hadn't seen yet. Even Asher gave Patrick sightseeing tips since they'd be traveling during the Christmas holidays.

He, on the other hand, was holding Abby in his lap and feeding her ice cream and the cake Amabelle had made for dessert. He should have thought to place a sheet over himself.

Abby laughed when he scrunched up his nose, then smiled when he winked. She'd touched his eyes when he stopped and clapped when he started winking again. The little thing spurred a dream he had so long ago. Children. A girl to be exact. One he could spoil. One he could give piggyback rides to. One he now wanted to look like Madi.

Brice grabbed a napkin and wiped Abby off, but she still looked as if she wore cake plastered to her shirt on purpose. He smiled to himself, not putting it past her. Nearing two years old, she was a handful.

Amabelle rose from the table and held out her hand to Abby. "Let's go and see if we can't find you a clean shirt."

Brice helped Abby down, and she ran up ahead. Her little feet pounded on the hardwood floors.

Asher leaned toward Madi. "Would you like to go for a walk?"

As if asking permission, she glanced at Brice. He looked away and rose from his chair, fully aware Patrick's eyes were on them.

"Sure." She smiled, but it seemed forced.

Brice carried his dishes from the table into the kitchen.

Patrick began piling the other dishes together when he returned. He nodded to Madi and Asher as they stepped off the patio, heading toward the woods. "Asher's been here since nine this morning anticipating this time with her."

Brice carried a few of the drink glasses to the sink and headed outside to the patio. She was almost out of view. He should give her room, as much privacy as he could, but her safety was his main concern. So he'd told himself repeatedly.

The back door opened, and Patrick stood alongside him. "I see the way you look at her. If I had my guess, I'd say you love her."

Brice remained silent.

"I wish I had fought for Amabelle years ago. She ended up falling for a guy a lot like Asher." He paused.

"All I'm saying is we both made mistakes, and in God's mercy, we found each other again, but sometimes that doesn't happen. There aren't always second chances."

"Asher has used your relationship with Amabelle as a way to win Madi back."

"At least he's fighting for what he wants." Patrick left him standing there.

Madi had long disappeared from his view, and he needed to go after her. His muscles tightened at the truth. If he went after her, it wouldn't be for the job, but to chase down the woman he loved.

He started down the path, his steps quickening. Since she'd walked into his life, he'd found contentment and peace, reassuring him that his new-found faith was indeed real. In realization, he stopped abruptly. Who else but the Lord knew what he needed, and then in His goodness, brought her into his life when he'd needed her the most.

Brice took off in a run. Seeing her with Asher in the distance, he slowed his steps for a calming breath and a plan. Walking up to them and kissing Madi straight on the mouth wasn't an option, and neither was telling Asher to take a hike because Madi was his girl.

His phone vibrated, stilling him. He grabbed his cell from his pocket and stared at the screen.

Adam.

****

For the life of her, Madi couldn't think of a way to let Asher know she wasn't interested in a relationship, but only in friendship. He was trying so hard, being so charming. That's what had drawn her to him in the first place. Now older and wiser, she was no longer tempted by charm. What tempted her was a man who believed in duty, pursued righteousness, and fought the evils of this world with courage, needing to make a difference.

But how would she convince Brice they belonged together? Because no matter how hard he was fighting it, he loved her. She was sure.

She glanced back, and Brice wasn't far behind.

Asher pointed ahead to the large rock they had spent hours playing on when they were kids—and making out on when they weren't. "It's hard to forget this place."

"We've had wonderful times here."

He took her hand and led her to the edge of the rock. "I've been useless, Madilyn. You're all I've been able to think of since I saw you last."

She inhaled and slipped her hand from his. "Asher…"

He dropped his head and jammed his shoe into the dirt. "It's him, isn't? Brice?"

"I'm sorry, Asher. For a moment there, it was nice to think about the way we were, but we aren't the same people. I have a career that I love and you hate. I couldn't give it up for you, and if I did, it would cause problems. Marriage can't be taken lightly, and if we did marry, it would be for the wrong reasons."

"Doesn't love count? Isn't it all that matters?"

"I used to think love was all that mattered, but I found sacrifice and commitment are just as important. I'm sorry. I can't settle for less."

"Madi!"

She turned to the urgency in Brice's voice. A light, giddy feeling came over her as he approached, but something about the way he moved didn't settle right.

Asher touched her arm, and she flinched. "You look surprised to see him. If he loves you in the same way you've fallen for him, I'm surprised he waited so long."

She frowned. "You knew?"

"I had hoped there was still something between us." Asher kissed her cheek and whispered, "Bye, Madilyn. I wish things were different. I will always love you."

Brice was now at their side, and he cleared his throat.

Asher straightened and released her. "Brice."

"I need to speak with Madi. Alone."

Brice's words came out harsh, but Asher nodded and looked to Madi. "See you at the wedding. Save a dance for me."

"I will." Madi smiled and tried to wait until Asher was farther down the path before commenting on Brice's behavior, but he wrapped his arm around her waist and pushed her into the woods. He stood so close, his face was only inches from hers. "Well, if you wanted a kiss, all you had to do was ask."

"This isn't the time, Madi. Something has happened. I need to get you home."

She pushed away from him, taking one step, then another, giving herself space to breathe and her heart time to settle. "We're safe here. Nobody knows about this place. I'm fine."

He schooled his features and met her gaze. "You can either walk out of here, or I'll carry you out. Your choice. But we *are* leaving."

And he would carry her, over his shoulder like a caveman if he had to. "All right. Where are we going?"

"Your place. Now come on." He snatched her hand and almost dragged her forward.

She yanked away and began to run. Brice was right on her heels.

When she reached the house, Brice held the door for her so she could enter. "Two minutes."

She knew what needed to be done. She pasted a perfect smile on her face and found Amabelle and Patrick on the couch, Abby playing with soft blocks on the floor. Asher was nowhere to be seen.

"Where's Asher?" she asked.

Patrick lifted Amabelle's hand and kissed her palm. "He's heading back to the hotel to change. We still have boxes to move from Amabelle's place before tomorrow's rehearsal dinner."

Amabelle gave a wide smile. "My last two nights in my home. I can't believe it."

"This is your home now." Patrick squeezed Amabelle closer, and she leaned against his chest.

Madi remembered what it was like next to Brice, the feel of him holding her. She had thought Brice was going to rescue her from Asher and declare how he felt, but she was sadly mistaken. Brice only went to her because it was his job. She was his responsibility.

No matter what she thought he might have felt, his actions were clear. He'd rather she be with Asher than with him. It was time to get it through her head. No more wishing. No more dreaming. "I think we're going to head out."

"You don't have to leave." Patrick moved his arms from Amabelle and stood.

Amabelle rose alongside him.

She hugged them both, but lingered at her brother's neck. "Actually, Brice and I have some things to talk about. I hope you don't mind."

"Of course not." Patrick looked to Brice and nodded. "Take care of my sister."

Brice led Madi to the door and grabbed her purse from the hook. "Always."

CHAPTER TWELVE

The sun blared in Madi's eyes, but it was Brice who lightened his grip on the steering wheel and flipped down his visor. He glimpsed her.

"Where's your ring?"

Madi realized then she'd been fingering a ring that wasn't there. She placed her hands in her lap and glanced out the window. "Left it at the house."

"Patrick's?"

"Mine."

"You're safe, Madi. What I said before I meant."

"I know."

Brice was silent the rest of the way to the house, and she found no reason to fill the void. Instead, she tried to understand what Adam's text meant and why they needed to leave.

Turning onto her street, Madi opened the garage door with her remote, and Brice pulled the car in. She unlocked the passenger-side door and hopped out before the garage completely closed, immediately sending Brice into motion. She ignored his stomping as he neared and stuck the key in the door, but Brice's firm grip on her waist stilled her.

"You'll wait for me," he ground out.

Irritation stirred her blood. "I don't need you to open the door. I think I can manage the menial task."

"As I'm sure you can, I'm entering first. You should have stayed in the car until I checked the grounds."

Grounds? This was a job to him. She didn't want to believe he'd been playing a part this entire time. Maybe that was her problem. She believed in those she loved. "This is my home and my life, though being here means nothing to you. If I want to go in first, I have every right."

"Then you'll have to go through me."

"Don't try me."

The door handle clicked, and within a blink, Brice grabbed her to his chest and spun them away from the entrance.

"You both get in here." Adam's voice rang clear. "I could hear you arguing from the living room." His steps carried away from them.

"Are you all right?" Brice's hushed tone filled her with yearning. The tightness of his embrace had yet to ease.

"Yes," she breathed, swallowing a lump in her throat. No matter how much she desired to stay where she was, she moved slightly and Brice released her.

Entering the house, she found Adam leaning over her kitchen counter. His dark forefinger sliding through her mail, separating each envelope one by one. "Adam, what are you doing here?"

"I knew a text and phone call wouldn't work." He continued to rummage through her mail. "When were you at the post office to pick up your mail?"

"I didn't. My brother's wife brought it to me yesterday when she picked up her daughter."

He looked to her then. "Your brother's married? I thought their wedding was the reason you didn't want to leave for an earlier flight to Vienna."

"They'll be married in two days."

Brice stood behind her. "You didn't come all this way to discuss her mail. What's going on?"

"You do have a P.O. box, correct?"

Her eyes narrowed. "Yes."

Adam tapped on the counter then met her gaze. "Who knew of this place?"

"No one except for my family."

"We've been partners for two years. I didn't even know." Brice agreed.

"Somehow Scott knew—"

"Scott?"

"We planned on prosecuting him and letting word get out that he was an undercover agent, but once he said he knew people and had certain connections, others stepped in. Higher ups."

"What are you saying?"

"He made a deal. They're freeing him tomorrow. He'll be working with the CIA."

Brice moved from behind her and stood near Adam. "Does your visit have to do with Scott?"

"Yes, and no. I was in Atlanta. Everything is set up for the meeting with Prince. At the end of the week, we'll have him and hopefully his girls."

"What does this mean for Constance?"

"I'm not sure right now, but because of Scott, I want you to leave, Madi. He made it a point to tell me he knew of this place. I don't trust him. Besides, I want you out of town when the meeting with Prince goes down. Being in Vienna early will give you a couple more days to scope out the area. Go sightseeing. I don't care."

"I'm not leaving, Adam. Like I told you before, this is my time to be with my family. I'm officially off duty, and the mention of Scott will not steal this time from me. I'm sorry."

He huffed. "Then stay, but I'm booking you both flights for the afternoon of the wedding. And in the meantime, you and Brice pack your things. Or I will personally pack you up myself."

"Yes, sir."

CHAPTER THIRTEEN

"Come on, Brice. Decorating for Christmas should be fun. I think I might start calling you Scrooge."

There was too much to think about. Scott, how he had learned where Madi's home was located. Madi's future as Constance, and what that might mean. The trip to Vienna with the woman he loved.

Decorating a tree was the last thing on his mind.

"Grab a hold of that end." Madi lifted Patrick's Christmas tree. "Won't my brother and Amabelle be surprised? I wish I could see their faces when they find the tree is up and decorated." She sighed wistfully.

Brice did as she asked and carried the seven-foot pre-lit tree into Patrick's living room and set his end by the window that faced the backyard. "Is this where you want it?"

"Perfect. Now let me get the lights." She headed back to the garage and he inhaled a long breath.

His world had been off its axis since he'd driven Madi to Georgia. He liked control, needed it during war, after the war, even with his constant battle with PTSD, but of all things, he needed it most in his relationship with Madi. If he could call it a relationship. Since Adam's visit, things automatically returned to the way they used to be with Madi. Partner, friends, but not a hint more. Perhaps her time with Asher yesterday had set their relationship in motion. He didn't want to think about how cozy they'd looked when he walked up on them.

Madi came back toting a green tub and set it to the floor. She lifted the lid, and boxes of lights stared back at him. "Wait a minute. It's a pre-lit tree. Why are we adding lights?"

"Those are white lights. These are colored. It gives them variety. They can use only one or both." She lifted several boxes from the tote. "I think this should do it."

It should. The tree would be a fire hazard after they got through with it.

She handed him a strand, and he held it out while she plugged them in to see if the lights were working. "Christmas really isn't your thing, is it? I kinda had a feeling last year at the Christmas party."

"Parents divorced right before Christmas when I was a kid. There wasn't much to celebrate that year or after. While on base though, I made sure we celebrated to help the men's morale. They missed their families, and I certainly could relate."

"You know there's another reason to celebrate Christmas, right? One reason that no matter what I might be facing, even now with the news of Scott, or that I feel like I'm being pushed to leave my family, keeps me in the right frame of mind."

"You're talking about Christ."

"Yeah. No matter what happens, I hold on to the fact that He came for me, to give me a hope and a future. The Lord helps me keep things in perspective when I can't see beyond today." She smiled up at him and pointed to the lights. "Can you hand me another box?"

After adding the extra lights and ornaments, Madi stepped back and admired their work. "What do you think? Like it?"

"It's great."

She met his gaze, a warm glow of happiness radiated from her. "Thank you for this. I know they will appreciate it as much as I do. I couldn't have done it in time without your help." She ran her fingers through her hair, then planted her hands on her slender hips. "It's beautiful."

She was beautiful.

He turned and began collecting the box of lights, ignoring the ache rising within him. After filling the tubs with empty ornament containers, icicles, and unused lights, they carried everything back into the garage. The happiness in Madi's gaze had yet to fade.

She was happy. It was all he wanted for her. Too bad it wasn't because of him. "Are you ready to head back? Tomorrow is the wedding, and we still need to pack up our things."

"Not really, but what choice do I have. Let me lock up and I'll meet you outside."

Brice went through the house, paused in the kitchen, and looked out to the living room, recalling the moments he'd shared with Madi's family. It had been a short couple of days, but he felt comfortable here. He enjoyed being a part of Madi's life and regardless of what she thought, everything about her mattered.

Madi came up behind him. "I thought you were waiting in the car."

"Are you ready?"

She unplugged the Christmas tree and glanced one last time at their work. "Sure."

Brice opened the passenger door for Madi and waited for her to slide in, but she paused. Her mouth opened to say something, but she closed it instead and lowered to the seat.

They drove back to Madi's in uncomfortable silence. So things hadn't exactly returned to normal between them.

A mile from the house, he decided to break the ice. "I never realized how important family and traditions are to you. Thank you for sharing them with me."

She looked up at him. "You're glad you came?"

"Yes, Madi. Honestly, I am. And I know leaving early isn't what you had planned."

She started biting the inside of her cheek. "It amazes me how people like Scott can just walk away. If it wasn't for him, I'd be staying." She glanced out the window. "I've been thinking. Adam was in Atlanta. He wasn't exactly nearby here in the mountains."

"He's concerned. I can't blame him. I am, too. The only difference between you and a civilian is you have the agency behind you. In a way, we're family."

"Is that why you've stayed with the agency so long? Family?"

"I guess so. And family is the reason I stay in touch with my buddies from Iraq and Afghanistan." He turned into their neighborhood. "Speaking of family, how is Asher taking the news of you leaving?"

"I haven't told him."

He drove into the driveway and stared at Madi as she pressed the garage door opener. "You haven't?"

She released her seatbelt as he inched his way into the garage and stopped. She got out of the car, and he sat there for a second before following her.

She turned and gave him a smirk. "I won't be tackled this time trying to open the door, will I?"

"As long as I enter first."

"Will it be this way in Vienna?"

"Yes. And no matter what you think is behind my motives, you will always be my main concern." He watched as she unlocked the door and gave him room to pass. He scanned the living room, kitchen, and went to her room. He recalled when he first brought her home. How things had changed in such a short time.

"Everything all right?"

No. Less than a week ago Scott tried to take Madi hostage. The possibility of losing her that night hit him all over again. "The night I brought you home, relief and fear seemed to strangle me. I almost lost you, Madi. As Scott drove down the highway, I could feel you slipping away. I'd never been so scared in all my life."

"But I'm here." She strolled a few steps in front of him. "I'm right here, but you're pushing me away."

"And I'm scared of losing you all over again, but this time to someone else. I almost interrupted you and Asher to tell you I was in love with you, but Adam called. When I finally reached you… it seemed you and Asher were close."

"Brice. There's nothing going on between Asher and me. All that happened was we talked briefly about the past, but mostly about you. Us. I told him the same as I told you, that I love you." She looked down to her hands. "My feelings can't be turned off and on. This isn't a game for me. Nothing has changed."

He was tired of fighting what he felt for Madi, but he was ready to fight any way he had to for a future with her. He reached out and cupped her cheek, running his thumb along her mouth. "What can I do to make this work between us?"

"Seek help for the PTSD and don't shut me out. Don't pull away when things get tough. I want to be by your side, like your buddies."

"I'm sorry, Madi." The distraught look on her face made him smile. "I can't see you in the same light. Those guys leave a lot to be desired compared to you."

She grinned and shook her head, placing a hand against his chest. "I want you to let me fight with you. I want to stay up late and watch the sunrise or sunsets when you need me to. I want you to trust me enough to let me in."

"I want to be able to promise you the world, Madi, but I'd be lying if I said this will be easy."

"When have I ever looked for easy? I fell in love with you, didn't I?"

He released a sigh and fingered the tips of her hair. "I want this with you. More than anything I've ever wanted in my life. But if I seek help for the PTSD, it will have to be on my own terms, without anyone knowing. If I do it any other way, they'll pull me from protecting you, and I can't let that happen."

"If they find out we're together, they'll pull us apart anyway."

"We'll be discrete." He stepped close and lifted her chin with his finger. Slowly, gently, he claimed her mouth. His heart was lost to her forever.

He rested his head against hers. "Protecting you is a job worth dying for; loving you is a gift worth living for, and I want both. To my very last breath."

CHAPTER FOURTEEN

Madi hurried to her seat and slid next to Brice. He smiled and leaned lightly against her shoulder. "I was afraid you weren't going to make it in time."

She lowered her voice to meet his. "They wouldn't have started without the bride. Oh, Brice, she looks stunning."

"The Wedding March" by Mendelssohn began to play, and they rose. Brice's hand settled along her back, and her heart warmed on contact.

Amabelle stepped down the aisle in rhythm to the music. Her Victorian-lace dress was breathtaking and fitted her slim figure to perfection.

Madi's heart swelled as she watched Patrick's expression upon seeing Amabelle. The width of his smile, the tears in his eyes. They were each other's soulmate.

She lowered to the bench with Brice at her side, and she fought to keep her mind on the ceremony, but every so often it wandered into the mystery of her own future.

Patrick placed the ring on Amabelle's finger. "I, Patrick, vow to remain faithful to you physically, emotionally, and spiritually, unto death do us part."

Madi swiped at a tear running down her cheek and continued to listen to their vows, the huskiness of Patrick's voice, the broken words of Amabelle that filled with emotion.

Amabelle slid Patrick's ring onto his finger. "I, Amabelle, vow to remain faithful to you physically, emotionally and spiritually unto death do us part."

Madi was still wiping away her tears when the pastor announced them as Mr. and Mrs. Reynolds. She stood and watched as her brother collected Abby from the pew and clasped Amabelle's hand before running down the aisle.

"They did it," she murmured, in awe of how God brought them to this moment.

Brice collected her hand and gave it a squeeze. "They did."

She looked to him, certain her own happiness was plain on her face. "You ready to celebrate? I feel like dancing. What do you say?"

"After we eat?" He wiggled his brows. "I've heard there's shrimp at the reception."

"Of course," she giggled as Brice led them from the pew.

The distance to the reception was only fifteen miles, yet the traffic caused long delays. She glanced at her cell and groaned in irritation. "We'll have less than two hours before we need to leave, and we aren't even there."

Brice reached over and cupped her hand. "We're almost there. We'll leave at the latest time possible. It will be all right."

And as if God answered her prayer without mouthing a word, the traffic cleared. A few minutes later, they pulled into the reception parking lot. "Isn't this place lovely? It's an old home built in the late 1800s."

Madi was eager to get out of the car, but waited for Brice. She tended to lead and move forward without thought, where Brice was the complete opposite. He contemplated his steps and planned his future. She smiled to herself. They were perfect for each other.

Brice opened her door and held out his hand. "I'm shocked you waited for me."

She placed her hand within his and stood. "It was difficult, but I managed."

He chuckled. "So it can be done. There is hope after all."

She took a step to him, and with both hands, she fixed his bow tie, meeting his gaze. "Don't get used to it. Tonight, I'll let you lead."

He laughed and pressed a kiss against her lips. "We'll see."

Madi found Patrick and Amabelle over in the corner of one of the living rooms speaking to several couples and many well-wishers. The line wound along the wall into the next room. Twenty minutes later, it was finally their turn. Madi grabbed Amabelle's neck in a hug. "Congratulations, my dearest friend. I'm so happy for you." Tears sprang to her eyes, and she pulled away quickly. "I don't want to get make-up on your dress. It's beautiful. You're beautiful." She swiped at her tears.

"Nonsense. It only adds to the memories."

Brice and Patrick were talking, but she interrupted with a hug. "Oh, brother, I'm so happy for you both. I just don't have the words."

"Me, either, sis. God is good. It's all I keep thinking."

She held him at arm's length. "Indeed, He is."

Patrick nodded to Brice. "You planning on taking my sister for a spin on the dance floor? It's time for our dance as husband and wife, but we hope you'll join us."

"We'd love to." Brice slid his arm around Madi's waist and led her to the edge of the dance floor.

She leaned her head to his chest. "I told you I'd let you

lead."

He kissed the top of her nose. "The night isn't over yet."

Madi and Brice swayed to the music as they enjoyed seeing her brother and Amabelle take their first dance together as Mr. and Mrs. Reynolds. It wasn't long though before Patrick pointed at Brice.

Without hesitation, Brice drew her to the floor and into his arms. It amazed her the way they seemed to float across the floor, the way each of their steps was marked with perfection as if they'd been dancing together their entire lives. She noticed it the first time they danced at the house, but now, as everyone was watching, she felt…she couldn't explain it. But when the song ended, and Brice met her gaze, she was sure he felt it too.

"You're amazing." His eyes darkened, and a smile lifted the corner of his mouth. "I can't wait to see what's in store for us in Vienna."

Neither could she.

Asher walked up to them. "Hey, Madilyn, may I have this next dance?"

Brice stepped away, and Asher took his place. Asher seemed to be watching her carefully.

She tilted her head and chuckled. "Do you have something on your mind?"

"I've never seen you this way."

"I've grown up, Asher. People change. I'm no longer the timid girl you used to know."

"I can see that I've missed out on so much." He cleared his throat. "I wish you both happiness."

"Thank you. That's all I've ever wanted for you."

"Promise me we'll keep in touch. We're family now." He smiled, taking her to the edge of the dance floor where Brice stood. "Take care of yourself."

Brice collected her within his arms as Asher walked away. "You okay?"

She swiped at another tear. "I guess I'm an emotional mess tonight."

"I'll take you any way I can."

She chuckled, wishing they were back at the house dancing alone. The way he was claiming her with his eyes and now holding her within his arms made moving almost impossible, breathing a struggle.

He whispered close to her ear. "It's time to go."

Madi understood it was, but she wanted this moment, the happiness she felt to last an eternity. The way they connected, the way they molded into each other, the oneness they shared from a single dance.

He kissed her hair. "You want to tell your brother goodbye one final time?"

She nodded, lost for words. She didn't know when she'd be back, but for her family's safety, she'd wait to return. But the memories of tonight she'd tuck away and hold close to her heart.

Tomorrow was a new day, a new beginning, one she hoped and prayed she'd gain with the man in her arms.

ABOUT THE AUTHOR

Tanya Eavenson is an international bestselling and award-winning inspirational romance author. She enjoys spending time with her husband and their three children. Tanya is a member of American Christian Fiction Writers. Her favorite pastime is grabbing a cup of coffee, eating chocolate, and reading a good book. To contact Tanya, visit her website at www.tanyaeavenson.com.